THE
HOPE OF
ELEPHANTS

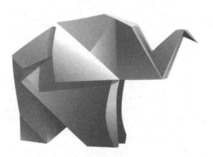

AMANDA RAWSON HILL

Emily Dickinson's "Faith is a fine invention" is reprinted in full on page 388 and "Hope"
is quoted in part on page 389, from Emily Dickinson, *Poems, Series Two*, Mabel Loomis
Todd and T. W. Higginson, eds. (Boston: Roberts Brothers, 1891) 53, 27 (public domain).

Robert Frost's "The Road Not Taken" is quoted in part on page 137, from
Robert Frost, *Mountain Interval* (New York: Henry Holt, 1916), 9 (public domain).

Sara Teasdale's "Barter" is quoted in part on page 470, from Sara Teasdale,
Love Songs (New York: Macmillan, 1918), 3 (public domain).

Dylan Thomas's "Do not go gentle into that good night" is quoted in part on page 343.
Excerpted under fair use from copyrighted material, from Dylan Thomas, *The Poems
of Dylan Thomas* (New York: New Directions, 1952, 2003), 239.

Published by Charlesbridge
9 Galen Street
Watertown, MA 02472
(617) 926-0329 • www.charlesbridge.com

Library of Congress Cataloging-in-Publication Data
Names: Hill, Amanda Rawson, author.
Title: The hope of elephants / Amanda Rawson Hill.
Description: Watertown, MA: Charlesbridge, [2022] | Audience: Ages 10 and up. |
    Audience: Grades 4–6. | Summary: "In this novel in blank verse, twelve-year-old
    Cass struggles to cope with her father's recurring cancers that have dominated
    her whole life, with the knowledge that he is likely to die soon because the latest
    recurrence is worse—and with the possibility that she may have inherited the genetic
    disease, Li-Fraumeni syndrome, that causes the cancers." Provided by publisher.
Identifiers: LCCN 2021029131 (print) | LCCN 2021029132 (ebook) |
    ISBN 9781623542597 (hardcover) | ISBN 9781632898463 (ebook)
Subjects: LCSH: Cancer—Juvenile fiction. | Genetic disorders—Juvenile fiction. |
    Death—Juvenile fiction. | Fathers and daughters—Juvenile fiction. | Grief—Juvenile
    fiction. | Narrative poetry. | CYAC: Novels in verse. | Cancer—Fiction. | Genetic
    disorders—Fiction. | Death—Fiction. | Fathers and daughters—Fiction. | Grief—
    Fiction. | LCGFT: Narrative poetry.
Classification: LCC PZ7.5.H55 Ho 2022 (print) | LCC PZ7.5.H55 (ebook) | DDC 813.6
    [Fic]—dc23
LC record available at https://lccn.loc.gov/2021029131
LC ebook record available at https://lccn.loc.gov/2021029132

Printed in China
(hc) 10 9 8 7 6 5 4 3 2 1

Illustrations done in Adobe Illustrator
Display type set in Blend Caps © Sabrina Mariela Lopez
Text type set in Adobe Minion Pro
Printed by 1010 Printing International Limited in Huizhou, Guangdong, China
Production supervision by Jennifer Most Delaney
Designed by Cathleen Schaad

For the Greenman family,
in memory of Diane, Kim, and
most especially Chris

PROLOGUE

There's a hill you have to climb
before you bike over the Golden Gate Bridge.
I did it when I was nine,
and it was so steep,
I wanted to quit right there.

But Dad wouldn't let me.
"This is all just part of the
experience," he said.

On the bridge, the wind whipped my hair
across my face.
It made my handlebars
wobble.
And I swear I felt the bridge
sway.
I wanted to get out of there.

But Dad wouldn't let me.
"This is a once in a lifetime
opportunity," he said.

Then halfway across,
the gray sky shifted and the sun broke through.
Light sparkled on the bay
like Christmas lights, glitter, and stained glass.
Beautiful.

CANCER

Cancer
visits my dad
in all the odd years
of my life,
no matter how much
we close the windows
and lock the doors.
It always finds a way to sneak inside.
It comes with different names,
but it's still
cancer.
When I was one it was
osteosarcoma.
Three:
colon cancer.
Five: brain.
Seven: colon again.
Nine was new. Testicular.
That's when I knew for sure
I'd be an only child—
the lone daughter.
Though we always knew
since the second round of chemo—
it would forever be
just me,
Mom,
Dad,
and cancer.
Always cancer.

So today,
my last day of eleven,
this odd year,
when I walk in the door
and see Mom and Dad
sitting on the couch,
I can tell
cancer is sitting there too.
It has
its own cushion,
its own sigh,
its own way of saying,
"Cass,
we need to talk."

I DIDN'T EVEN KNOW

I didn't even know Dad was sick,
or thought he was sick,
or felt something.
However a diagnosis starts.
I rack my brain
wondering
if I missed the signs.
Long glances at the dinner table?
Whispered conversations
behind closed doors?
That sticky feeling
between two people who are
keeping a secret together—
away from me.
But all I remember is
folding
paper cranes for an hour with Jayla.
Catching
that perfect pop fly at baseball.
Riding
past the park with the wind in my face,
my hair
whipping past my ears.

QUESTIONS

There are questions
people ask
when you say the word.
Cancer.
Asked so many times
that if questions could cause tumors,
my dad would be dead by now.
Where?
What stage?
How long does he have?
They don't realize
that answering
is like chemo.
The question is gone,
but we're still poisoned.
The answers are the tricky,
never sure,
knock-on-wood kind
anyway.
There are only two
truly important questions.
So I ask.
"What about baseball?"
Mom sighs.
"I don't think . . ."
She stops.
"I mean,
your season's almost over anyway."

"Four-fifths,"
I say,
picking
at my sleeve.
"It's four-fifths of the way over.
Can't I at least go
until Dad starts treatment?"
Mom sighs again, then says,
"Practice is tomorrow,
but we have meetings with the doctors all day,
plus it's your birthday.
Then Dad has to get blood tests
on Saturday.
They're scheduled during your game.
I'm sorry, Cass.
I already called your coach."
Her decision lands at my feet
like a missed catch,
just lying on the ground between us.
I want to pick it up.
Try throwing it again.
But instead I ask
the second important question.
"Will we miss the World Series?"
"Never," says Dad,
cracking a grin at the thought.
Finally an answer I want.

BASEBALL

I never wanted to play baseball.
Not before Dad took me outside.
Put the glove on my hand,
showed me how to hold it high above my head.
A gentle toss.
Ball on the ground.
Over and over.
"Can we be done now?" I whined.
"Keep your eye on the ball."
That's all he said.
And then finally.
One moment,
eyes up,
the *thunk*
of my first catch.
I've been hooked ever since.

THE WORLD SERIES

Dad writes a blog
that lots of people read.
About
cancer
and family
and life—and
cancer.
I don't know why,
but people like reading about it.
About being sick.
When I was four,
he wrote about how fighting
a disease
is like baseball.
Everybody loved it.
They loved it so much,
they sent our family to the World Series.
Just me, Mom, and Dad.
I guess it's not only little kids
who have big wishes that get granted.

Dan's Tires,
the place Dad worked all through college,
remembered him
and promised
to send us every year for the rest of Dad's life.
They probably thought that would be
only a few years.
Now we've been
eight times.

Eight times sitting in a stadium.
Eight times eating nachos.
Eight times cheering for the underdog (like us).
Eight times sitting by my dad.

There's nothing much better than watching a game
next to someone who's supposed to be dead,
but instead he's singing
"Take Me Out to the Ball Game."

TICK TOCK

Mom and Dad lean forward on the couch.
Watching me.
As if they're waiting for me to say something else.
Something more.
But what is there to say?
We've been through this before.
It always turns out okay.
It may be hard
and lonely
and scary,
but
Dad will be okay.
Right?

The clock on the wall echoes
the chant in my head.

Tick.   *Tock.*
Tick.   *Tock.*

O.   Kay.
O.   Kay.

Base.   Ball.
Base.   Ball.

MOM'S SMILE

Her smile is worn thin,
wrinkled around the corners,
and glued on.
A paper smile.

CAN I GO?

I jump up from my chair.
Need to leave.
Need to get out.
Get away
from cancer and its smirking smile.
The clock
ticking away my questions.
Over and over.
Mom and Dad watching me,
waiting for
what?
"I just need . . . some alone time."

Mom frowns.
"I thought we'd have some family time—"
Dad interrupts her.
"Let her go.
She'll be getting plenty of family time
soon enough."
I rocket out of there
faster than
a major-league pitch.

UNDER THE FLOWERING CHERRY

The cherry tree in the park across the street
begins the spring
pink,
fluffy,
flowered.
Turns green in summer.
Blazes out in fall—
deep red,
almost purple.
Maroon.
They're dark green now—
the leaves.
I lie beneath them,
thinking.
I used to search for fairies here.
Now I come
to fold little paper birds
like the ones I see in the branches.
Fold,
unfold,
crease,
bend,
pray.

Until a robin appears—
from my prayer
and a paper square.
And I wonder
for just a second
where I would go if I had wings.
Somewhere far, far away.

Venice?
Ukraine?
Or maybe close by.
Baseball practice?
My games?
If I had wings . . .

I feel a kick on the sole of my shoe.
Look up.
It's Dad.
He hands me a glove.
Says, "Let's go."
And we do.

FOR BASEBALL

The ball

zooms between us

saying so much

that words can't.

Like a song,

a meditation,

a daydream,

a chant.

Sunset falls,

the field goes dark.

We wait for a moment

till the lights turn on with a spark.

Dad smiles at me, throws,

and then calls.

It's never too late.

It's never too late.

It's never too late

for baseball.

THE PITCH

We lie on the grass.
Gloves off,
stars above us,
mosquitoes biting through our clothes.
Dad goes first,
like he always does with this tradition.
"So, Cass," he says.
"Tell me something I don't know."
I let the air in my lungs out
slowly,
like a long, low
hisssss.
A ball deflating.
I'm winding up
to pitch Dad the idea that's
rolling around in my brain.
"I'm going to be twelve tomorrow."
"I already know that," Dad says.
"I think that's old enough
for me to get myself
to baseball practice."
Dad rolls onto his side.
The grass quietly rustles beneath him.
"What do you mean?"
The ball releases from my hand.
                    It's in the air.
                              No turning back.

"I mean,
the field is only
seven blocks away.
Sidewalks the whole way.
Protected crossings.
I know how to do it.
I can get there on my bike
in like
ten minutes.
Tops.
I'm . . .
I'm not a baby anymore.
I can do it."
Dad lets out a sound:
sssshhhhheeewwww.
I wait.
Wait to see if my ball connects with a bat.

        Wait to hear what he'll say back.

THE REPLY

Finally he whispers,
"You're right."
"Really?"
I sit up so fast,
my head gets dizzy.
"Absolutely," says Dad.
"You should get to finish your season.
You shouldn't have to quit because of
your dumb ol' dad."
"You're not dumb."
He smiles.
A sad smile.
"This body of mine sure is."
I don't say anything about that.
But when he stands up,
I squeeze him hard around the middle.
"Thank you,
thank you,
thank you!"
He hugs me back.
Chuckles.
Then says,
"Let me break the news to your mom, all right?"
On our way back home,
I finish the tradition.
"Hey, Dad.
Tell me something I don't know."
He stops right in front of
our apartment door.

Puts his hands on
my shoulders and says,
"Cass,
everything's going to be okay."
The words are like flashlight beams
in the darkness.
I smile.
"I already knew that."

GROUP EMAIL

I pull out my laptop and start typing
a quick email.
Nothing too long
or dramatic.
Keep it short and breezy.
Hey guys,
Looks like I'll be back at group therapy soon.
Anything exciting happen while I was away?

I close the computer
and wish
Blaine's mom would let him have a phone.
Texting would be so much easier.
I imagine Blaine,
Elena,
and Jazz reading my message,
knowing how they'll reply.

With something short,
funny,
and without an ounce of pity.
When parents have had cancer
as long as ours have,
there's not a drop of that
left.

FAMILY HOME EVENING

It's Monday, which means
Family Home Evening.
Dad opens the scriptures—
the blue book with gold writing on the cover—
and reads the same story he always reads
when cancer comes to visit.
The one about the three boys,
the king,
and the furnace of fire.
They believed God would save them, and then said,
"But if not."
I don't know why Dad likes that part so much.
How can he love a scripture that says
God might not save you?
He closes the book and smiles.
Mom shakes her head and says,
"I'm so grateful we have the chance to fight this,
to grow our faith
and draw closer together."

I think Mom would say that even in front
of a real fiery furnace.

Me?
I'd ask for a fire extinguisher.

I WAIT

I wait
for Dad to give my pitch to Mom.
I figure he'll lob it to her
slow,
underhand,
nice and easy.
But he never says anything about it.
Not one thing.
Maybe he'll mention it
when I'm in bed
and can't hear.
Or maybe he'll forget.

TEXT TO JAYLA

Jayla is my best friend.
And every night
as we get ready for bed,
we send a message.
Want to try Berlin tonight?
I pull up Google Earth.
    What street?
Hinter der Katholischen Kirche.
I find it.
    By the domed cathedral?
Yes.
    There's a lot of trailers parked around it.
    It's under construction.
That way we won't end up at any old cathedral.
I'll meet you there tonight.

Jayla and I like to think that if we concentrate
before we fall asleep,
we can meet in the same spot
in our dreams.
It hasn't worked yet.
But you never know.
It might.
We can't leave home yet—
can't fly away—
but in our dreams . . .

and one day for real.

SHAKESPEARE

Dad reads me poetry
before I go to sleep.
He calls it bonding.
Mom calls it language arts.
He used to read Shel Silverstein.
But a few months ago,
he said it was time to move to harder stuff.
Lately it's Shakespeare.

Like as the waves make towards the pebbl'd shore,
So do our minutes hasten to their end.

I tell Dad I don't like this one.
"Just let it finish, Cass," he replies.
"Give the bard a chance.
You know I'll explain it to you."
But I don't need Dad to explain.
"Please, Dad. Just Shel Silverstein tonight."
He sighs.
Reads me "Hug of War."
Which means, of course,
we have one too.
Mom even joins in,
though she says she's not on either team.
We laugh,
pull away.
Mom lights a candle.
Sings.
Tells me to pray.

MY DAD IS A CANDLE

Some people believe every life
is a flame.
A candle waiting to be
snuffed out.
If my dad is a candle,
I think he's a trick one.

MY FOURTH WORLD SERIES

We sat in a foul ball area.
Mitts out,
eyes open,
breath held.
The balls fell into the bleachers,
and the people
zoomed to get them.
I worried.
What if I wasn't fast enough?
Got hit in the head?
It never happened,
but every time I heard the
CRACK!
of a bat,
I covered my eyes anyway.
Until Dad pried my hands
off my face
and said,
"If you're scared the whole time, Cass,
you'll miss the best parts."

TWELVE

Today I am twelve.
It's an important number.
Twelve.
Twelve eggs in a dozen.
Twelve apostles.
Twelve tribes of Israel.
Twelve inches in a foot.
Twelve hours on a clock.
Twelve months in a year.
Twelve years in my life.
In Scotland, I could write my own will.
If I were Jewish, I'd have a bat mitzvah.
It's the last year before I'm a teen.
And the first year I can have pierced ears,
wear lip gloss,
and ride the train all by myself.
It's why I've moved out of Primary
and into Young Women's at church,
with the older girls who wear
makeup that's too grown-up for me,
shoes that are too tall for me,
and bras that I don't think I'll ever really need.

It's an important number.
Twelve.

CHECK MY PHONE

It's so early, but
there's already a text
from Jayla.
*Happy Birthday! Did you know in China you're
supposed to eat really long noodles? And slurp
them up the way my mom hates! Maybe we should
go to China.*

Jayla and I are planning a trip.
The day we're both eighteen,
we'll hop on a plane
and get the heck out of here,
as Jayla likes to say.
Jayla really wants to go to Africa.
She wants to get back
to her family's roots.
I've been pushing for Asia for at least
a month, though.
So I text back.
    That's what I've been CHINA tell you.
    Get it?

BIRTHDAY TRADITIONS

Every year on my birthday,
Mom puts up streamers
and a cascade of balloons that fall from my door
like a waterfall.
But today there is none of that.
Only scurrying like mice,
opening cupboards for breakfast,
and cancer
sitting on a stool next to Dad.
"Happy birthday," says Dad.
"You get to go to the hospital."
I try to smile.
"Just what I always wanted."
He squeezes my shoulder.
Whispers, "I'm so sorry."

Mom rushes in.
"Cass, I'm so sorry.
With everything that happened yesterday,
I forgot all about balloons.
But tonight we'll celebrate.
Sound good?"
I nod,
check my phone,
mess with a loose thread.
Anything to not look
cancer
in the face.

Because it's smiling at me,
the way it always does when it ruins something.

PACKING

I pack my backpack
with books and my baseball glove
and cleats. Just in case
Dad never asks Mom. And I
have to do this on my own.

EMAIL FROM ELENA

It comes in right
before we leave.
Surprise, surprise.
You just couldn't stand
not being one of the cool kids.
Could you?
As far as anything new at therapy . . .
nobody's mom has died for like
four months.
So that's different. 🙂

HOPE CIRCLE

The road in front of the hospital
is called Hope Circle.
It sounds nice when you first see the sign.
Hope.
It makes your insides feel like toasted
marshmallows.
But then you read
the second word.
Circle.
A circle never ends.
You always come back
to where you started.
So I don't see how they can call this circle
Hope
when we keep coming back to the very place
we never want to see
again.

IN THE PARKING GARAGE

Dad stands
with his hands
on the car.
"I just need to breathe," he says,
"before I walk back in there."
Mom and I understand.
We need to breathe too.
So
we wait
till he's ready.
Finally he whispers,
"Once more unto the breach."

And we go.

OLD FRIENDS

The hospital is filled
with old friends.
They know us by name,
wave us through,
comment on how tall I've grown.
They pat Dad on the back and say,
"I was hoping I'd never see you again."
Dad doesn't laugh.
He just says, "Me too."

NURSE HEATHER

Nurse Heather
walks along
with white shoes,
purple scrubs,
ponytail.
She sees me,
wipes her eyes,
walks over,
pulls me in,
holds me tight,
squeezes hard,
whispers low,
"I have lunch
in an hour.
Meet you there."
Then she lets go.

MY SIXTH WORLD SERIES

Outfield,
right field,
center field.
Doesn't matter.
These were the worst seats ever.
We watched the game on a screen.
"Might as well be at home,"
I complained.
Until
Dad took me to get garlic fries
at the stand right below our seats
with hardly any line.
Those were the best fries I've ever eaten.

"See?" Dad said. "There's something good
in every situation."

TEXT FROM JAYLA

We could go to Vietnam.
Everyone there celebrates their birthday
on the same day.
We would be twins!
I smile as I walk
down the sparkling clean halls,
machines beeping in every room.
    That sounds like Syrias fun.
Jayla texts back.
Okay, that was Nepal-ing.
I laugh,
then remember where I am.
Put my phone
and my smile
away.

EMAIL FROM JAZZ

u can run,
but u can't hide.
#CancerKidsForLife
haha but srsly.
have we tried
running
or hiding yet?
it might help.

BOOKS

I always bring books to the hospital.
Books for fun with broken spines
from reading over and over.
Books for studying
whatever I feel like learning.
Books to read in one sitting.
Books to savor.
Books to keep me from having
to talk to anyone I don't know.
Books to keep me from hearing
what the oncologists say.
Today it's *The Vanderbeekers*
with pages falling out.
But the doctor is talking, and
I can't stop listening.
No matter what Isa or Jessie says,
the doctor's words are louder.
Treatment plan.
Chemo.
Radiation.
Genetic testing.
Mom cries,
"What?"
and looks at me.
Cancer laughs,
and I close the book.

WHY CANCER'S ALWAYS HERE

I lean forward in my chair.
The doctor notices I'm listening.
"Your father has a gene," he says.
"Or really, he lacks a gene. It's mutated."
He wipes sweat from his forehead
and continues to
explain
until it's finally clear
why cancer's always here.
Dad's body doesn't know
how to close the windows,
lock the doors—
tell cancer to bug off.
That's why it moves in every other year,
makes itself at home.
Blows, and blows, and blows
at Dad's little flame.
"I have some pamphlets," the doctor says.
He pushes a gray-and-green one at my dad
and one with elephants on the front
toward me.

But I am not a baby
who needs elephants to tell me
why my dad is always
almost
dying.

"There is something else," says the doctor.
"Something I should speak to you about
in private."

IN PRIVATE

When grown-ups say
"in private"
and shoo you out the door,
it can mean one of three things.

1. They are talking about something scary.
2. They are making decisions they don't want you
   to know about.
3. They are talking about you.

My hand slips on the doorknob
as I let myself out,
because I think
this time
it might be all three
at once.
And if it is,
I should get to stay.
I look back
one last time.
They all smile and nod me toward the door.
Get out of here, they're thinking.
You're too young.
I spy another one of the
pamphlets
the doctor gave my dad
and sneak it into my backpack on the way out.

I am not a baby.

OUTSIDE THE OFFICE

I sit on the bench across the hall
and toss the elephant pamphlet
to the ground.
Whatever the doctor is telling my parents,
it won't be found
in something that doubles as a coloring book.
I pull out the gray-and-green one
and begin reading.

There are a lot of big words.
But I understand most of it.
Dad hasn't been reading me
Shakespeare
for nothing.

It talks about genes.
(The p53 gene.)
And mutations.
(There's something called Li-Fraumeni syndrome.)
And a test that shows if you are
positive or negative for it.
(Dad tested positive.)

And lots and lots of numbers.

The odds of having the gene.
(One in twenty thousand.)
The risk of women with the gene getting cancer
before the age of thirty.
(Fifty percent.)

The risk for men.
(Twenty percent.)

My dad must have
terrible,
awful
luck.

And then one paragraph stops me.
I have to read it
again.

WHAT IT SAYS

The mutated gene is autosomal dominant.
Fifty percent of children born to parents with
Li-Fraumeni syndrome will also have the mutation.

I have to read it again. Because I think,
It's talking about me.
Children born to parents with Li-Fraumeni.
My dad has Li-Fraumeni—
the doctor says he does—
so I
am a child born to a parent
with Li-Fraumeni.
Fifty percent
of children
like me
will also have the mutation.
The mutation is . . .
The gene is . . .
Li-Fraumeni is . . .
I press the pamphlet to my chest
to try to slow my heart's sharp
beating.

Fifty percent of girls with Li-Fraumeni syndrome
will be diagnosed with cancer
by the time they're thirty.

Fifty percent.

Fifty percent.

Thirty.

When my mom was thirty,
I was five.

When I'm thirty I'm . . .

       . . . supposed to have flown   away

and come back
and flown away some more.

Fifty percent.
Fifty percent.

50/50

50/50
works for
a lot of things.
Coins.
Babies.
Odd numbers.
But I am none of those.
I'm just a girl
with a dad who is unlucky.
It's a fifty-fifty chance
that I'm unlucky too.

And suddenly,
I'm   split
in   two.
Positive.   Negative.
With the gene.   Without the gene.
Cancer.   Health.
Invalid.   Traveler.
Two   futures.
Two   paths.
Two   of

me.

POSITIVE & NEGATIVE

This is the side of me—
the path of me—
without a future.
Or at least,
with a fifty-percent chance
of cancer by thirty.
And then cancer again
and again
and again.
Instead of all the plans
I have.
Instead of all the dreams
I dream.

This is the side of me
with a future—
wide open.
Nothing known.
Like a song,
the first time you hear it,
a blank sheet of paper,
an unread book.
A promise.

FOR ME

I know what they're talking about
in that tiny office.
What the doctor is saying.
I can picture them now.
Dad with his head in his hands.
Mom with her paper smile
looking for something—
anything—positive
about this.

My stomach tightens.
Hands shake.

Back to the pamphlet.
It mentions a test.
A test to know for sure.
But as I find that part again,
I think of Dad,
just needing to breathe.
Once more unto the breach.

My breath catches.
Knuckles turn white.

I pick up the elephant pamphlet off
the floor and put both in my backpack
and think of Shakespeare.

CHOICE

To know or not to know, that is the question.
Whether it's better to suffer life knowing
that disease and treatments are sure to come,
or to float on a sea of chances.
To fight back or to lie back. Wait for cancer
if cancer ever dares to show its face here.
To live a life of dreams.
Dreams.
Ay, there's the rub.

THE DOOR OPENS

Mom and Dad walk out.
There are tissues balled up in their hands.
Mom sniffs.
Dad's eyes are red.
I stand and wait for them to look at me,
their broken daughter
split down the middle.

It feels like an hour passes—
maybe two—
while they stand there staring at me.
The second hand on the clock ticks
one,
two,
three,
four.
And even though the hall is filled with words,
monitors,
and shuffling feet,
there is only silence between us
while I wait for them to say it.
Just say it.
We have some bad news.

BREAKING THE ICE

Breaking the ice,
that's what people call it
when you're meeting someone new
and looking
for the right thing to say.
I am not someone new
to my parents.
But I feel changed.
Different.
Do they see it?

I break the ice.

"What did the doctor say?"
And just like that,
Mom's paper smile is back.
"Oh, nothing.
Grown-up stuff."

It is a silent,
earth-shattering,
instantaneous
crack in the ice.

We are drifting
in opposite directions
across a frozen sea.

THE LONG WALK

"Well," says Mom,
"let's get you to your lunch date."
Dad's hand is on my back.
He leads me down the hallway to the elevator.
Mom talks and talks and talks
about nothing.
Absolutely nothing.
How can she talk about nothing with all this
something
swirling around us?
And even on the elevator,
our bodies crammed in tight,
shoulder to shoulder,
head to chest,
I feel
a million miles away.
On the sixth floor
I stop at the door to the cafeteria.
I look at Dad.
"Tell me something I don't know."
Dad looks at Mom, who just smiles.
She smiles!
And she says, "I'm adding an extra surprise
to your birthday brownies tonight."

Dad clears his throat.
Stares at the floor.

Okay, fine, if they won't treat me
like I'm old enough to talk about this,
I know someone who will.

LUNCH

Nurse Heather
is sitting
and waiting
with her lunch.
I sit down.
She gives me
a cupcake,
smiles and says,
"I know it's
not the best
twelfth birthday.
But maybe
this will help."
My mind's stuck
on before.
I shake the
thoughts away.
"You really
remembered?"
I ask her.
"Of course I
remembered.
It's my half
birthday too."
She pushes
the cupcake
closer still
and waits for
me to eat.

CUPCAKE

The frosting is red.
Probably has
red dye 40
or red number 3.
Carcinogens both,
things that can cause cancer.
I know
from when Mom went on a kick,
trying to keep Dad from getting sick again.
Which seemed silly then,
but not so much anymore.
It looks like a cupcake, but really,
it's a doorstop,
a window prop,
a way to let cancer in
through all the entrances
I can't close.

The frosting is red,
swirled perfectly
to look almost
like a rose.
There are tiny
silver sprinkles.
The wrapper is
a sunny
yellow.
I rip it off.
Underneath
the cake is a rich brown.
Spongy and moist.
Ready for my first
bite.

With crumbs between my teeth,
in my lap,
on my hands,
I finally look
at Nurse Heather
and tell her everything.
About my dad
and his genes
and my genes.

About the
two sides of me
and the knowing,
and not knowing
the future
and the past.
How one test
could change everything.

Could tell me exactly
where
I
am
headed.
And the two sides of me
that don't know

if that's good

or bad.

HOW DO YOU FEEL?

Nurse Heather
listens, frowns.
"I'm really
sorry, Cass.
What do your
parents think
you should do?"
"I wouldn't
know," I say.
"We haven't
exactly
talked about
it all yet."
She says, "Well,
how do you
feel about
all of it?"

HOW DO I FEEL?

There was this game a year ago
where my team was down one run
in the bottom of the ninth.
Two outs.
I was on second
with another runner on third.
Jack was up at bat—
hit the ball
far
into left field.
It bounced along the grass,
evading the catch.
I ran.
Third base coach told me,
"Keep going.
All the way home."
That meant we were tied.
If I could get home,
we'd win!
I slid
into the plate.
Felt my fingers graze the rubber
just before
the catcher's mitt slammed
against my arm.
I was safe.
I knew it.
We won!

But the ump jerked his hand.
Yelled, "Out!"

"No!"

But there's no arguing in baseball.
No instant replays
in Little League.
No way to make my case—
to make him believe that I'd felt the base.
I was safe,
and then I was out.
We'd won, but
then it was extra innings.
And we lost.

The feeling I have now
is the same.
I was safe,
and now I'm not.

We were winning,
and now it's extra innings
in a game that will never
ever
end.

PROS AND CONS

Nurse Heather
nods and frowns.
"It's so hard,"
she whispers.
"And it's not
fair at all.
But if you're
not ready
to talk to
your parents
about the
test, what if
you write up
a list of
pros and cons?
Whichever
side's longer,
that is your
solution.
Every choice
comes with a
consequence.
You decide
what you can
live with knowing
or not
about yourself."

This sounds far
more honest
than what Mom
and Dad have
been trying
to do to
me today.
Easier
to focus
on something
visible,
countable,
reasons for
here and now.
She tears off
a piece of
paper from
her notepad
and hands it
to me with
her pen. I
start writing.

PROS AND CONS OF GETTING TESTED

Pros

Cons
1. It might be more bad news.

TAP

Nurse Heather takes her pen
and taps the blue cap.
"Yes it could be bad news,
but it could be good news too."
I sigh.
Two paths.

PROS AND CONS OF GETTING TESTED

Pros
1. It might be good news.

Cons
1. It might be more bad news.

EMAIL FROM ELENA

Haven't tried running or hiding.
But my mom has us all
on a new diet.
No sugar,
no butter,
no milk,
no peanuts,
no meat.
My whole life is zucchini.

I can't laugh
even though it should be funny.
But I type a reply real fast.
Been there.
Didn't help.
I'll sneak some brownies to the next group session.

My email dings a minute later.
I know I shouldn't say this, but
I'm glad you're coming back.
She's right.
She shouldn't say it.
But we still do.

CAR RIDE HOME

Mom's eyes flicker in the rearview mirror.
From me to Dad, back to me.
She tries to smile,
but it comes out as a grimace.
Finally she asks,
"Is something wrong, Cass?"
I roll the window down—
then up.
But I do not speak.
I wait for them to tell me,
to talk to me about my life,
my genes,
my test.
Instead Dad leans forward,
holds his head in his hands.
"I'm so, so sorry."

Is he talking about my gene?

Mom hushes him like a baby.
"It's not your fault. Cass understands."

Is she talking about my gene?

"We'll still have a party tonight. Won't we, Cass?"

My birthday.
She's talking about my birthday.
Her eyes flash in the mirror back to me.
And they seem to be asking a question.
You're okay, right?

WHAT I DON'T SAY

My birthday's ruined,
and you're keeping secrets. Well,
two can play that game.

WHAT I ACTUALLY SAY

"Yeah. I'm just fine.
Can I go over to Jayla's
when we get home?"

"It's your birthday. I thought we'd—"
Mom sighs. "Yeah. Okay. I guess."

TEXT TO JAYLA

I type.
    Maybe we should go to Mexico.
    I wouldn't mind
    smacking
    a piñata right now.
Jayla texts back.
What's wrong?
What Canada for ya?
I reply quickly.
    Just be ready for me.
    I'm coming over.
She types quickly too.
I can't wait!
I'll be Czech-ing the door.

It's nice
to have a best friend
who can always make me giggle
even when I want
to kick
and punch
and scream.

MY SEVENTH WORLD SERIES

My only goal that year
was to get on the Jumbotron.
Mom and Dad were happy to help me
with face paint,
a ridiculous hat,
and a giant foam finger.

"You have to be over the top," said Dad.
"You have to be adorable," said Mom.
"She's always adorable," said Dad.

So the whole game, I danced
and shouted
and cheered.
Like I was the home team's
number-one fan,
even though I don't actually have
a favorite team.
I like all of them.

Then finally,
up on the screen,
there I was.
Kind of.
Half of me was
poking into the frame
that held Mom and Dad
and the words
KISS CAM.

All my silliness,
all my trying,
while Mom and Dad just sat there
and laughed,
and they got chosen?

Dad grabbed my hand,
pulled me between them,
and they both
kissed me on a cheek.

The crowd went wild.

BIKE RIDE

Grab my helmet.
Put it on straight.
Push it down hard.
Clip the buckle.
Pull the straps.
No empty space.
No wiggle room.
Must do it right.
Follow the rules.

There's something about
running away,
even for an hour,
that makes the wind move faster
past my ears.
Rushing,
whooshing,
flying.

The cars speed past.
I pedal faster.
Pamphlets and baseball gear
in my backpack
reminding me
of all that I can lose.

JAYLA'S HOUSE

It takes a while for Jayla to answer
when I knock on her door.
She finally opens it and says,
"Happy birthday!"
Jayla pulls a card
from the mail holder on the wall.
Her mouth doesn't stop moving.
"This took me forever.
I kept messing up
and had to start over
and over.
But I finally got it just right.
You're going to love it."
The outside is thick.
Cardstock.
Deepest black.
I open it up.
Inside a white paper castle
POPS up!
"Hogwarts,"
I whisper.
Jayla grins and begins
to point out the turrets
and windows.
"The astronomy tower was hardest."
I whisper
because I can hardly find my voice,
"I love it."
And for the first time today,
it actually feels like a birthday.

PAPER ENGINEERING

It takes careful hands
to be a paper engineer.
That's what Jayla and I are.
We bend
and fold,
cut
and glue.
Over and over.
Changing paper into
anything—
into everything.
It's tricky,
tiny,
tiring work.
It requires patience.
That's why Jayla and I
are so good at it.
Everything in our lives
has made us more
patient
than most people.
So we fold
and cut.
Bend
and glue.

Wait
and dream.

LESSONS

"Finished your schoolwork?"
Mrs. Jasper calls.
"Yes," says Jayla.
Whispers "no" to me.

She wants me to laugh.
I don't.
"Everything okay?"
"I don't know," I say.

"Come finish your math!"
her mom calls.
Jayla sighs and says, "Come on."

I walk down the hall
even though math seems pointless
on days like today.

SCHOOL

Schools have
playgrounds,
kids,
teachers,
chalkboards,
desks,
worksheets,
grades,
timed tests.
You have to
be like everyone else.
Walk in a straight line.
You can't be
too loud,
too questioning,
too energetic,
too far behind,
too far ahead.
You can't have a hard time
with crowds,
loud noises,
or things going off schedule.
That's why Jayla's twin brother
is homeschooled.
And Jayla with him.
People say schools have lots of problems.
But most of all
schools have lots and lots
of germs.

Germs that travel home on backpacks,
hands, and pencils
and make people sick.
People like my dad.
That's why I
started off homeschooled.
I still am because
I like it.

I like deciding
what I want to learn:
like rocketry, mythology,
and Korean cuisine.
Where I want to learn:
the library, the zoo,
a park bench, my bed.
And when I want to learn too.
Like studying all through
the hot months of summer
so we can take a three month break
from Thanksgiving to Valentine's.

You can't do that in a school.

LEARNING

Jayla's brother, Alex,
leans over their piano,
carefully pressing each key with perfect precision.
A melody all too familiar
comes out.
Alex's favorite song for the past month,
played so many times
he doesn't need to even look
at the music anymore.
Jayla sits on the couch,
uses the postcard I sent from
the Series in San Francisco
to mark her place in
1,000 Places to See Before You Die.
Pulls out her math book.
"What's up?"
she asks while her pencil scratches away.
I tell her
in hushed tones,
because it is still
my secret.
But somewhere in the middle of my story,
Alex stops playing
and starts listening to my words like they
whistle,
pop,
buzz.
When I get to the end,
Jayla's eyes are wide.
She shakes her head.
"Oh, Cass . . ."

SCHRÖDINGER'S CAT

"Whoa!"
interrupts Alex.
"You might have a mutated gene?
Which chromosome?
What's the hereditary graph for that?
Dominant? Recessive?"
Alex walks over to the whiteboard
hanging on their wall,
erases what he was working on,
and begins writing letters,
symbols,
my name.
"You know what this reminds me of?"
says Alex.
"Schrödinger's cat."
He looks away from the board,
stares at me.
Because suddenly,
I'm like a new piece of music
or an equation.
Something interesting
pounding at the door.
"Dead and alive at the same time."

"Stop it," says Jayla.
"Schrödinger's cat," he whispers.
"What," I ask,
"is Schrödinger's cat?"

SCHRÖDINGER'S CASS

Once there was
a scientist
named Schrödinger,
who had a theory
about a cat.
A cat in a box.
A box filled with poison
that will kill the cat.
But only at
a certain time
that nobody can
predict.
And until that box
is opened
the cat is both

dead   and   alive

because until you know for sure,
it can be
either answer.
Just like me.
Schrödinger's Cass.

TRAPPED

There are two sides of me.

Cancer.	Health.
Death.	Life.
Stuck at home. Sick.	Traveling the world. Free.

And I'm trapped
in the box,
and I claw
at the sides.
I don't know
which I am.
I don't get
to decide.
I won't know till
I open
the box.
Am I stuck
or will I fly?
Am I dead
or alive?

SOMETHING ELSE

"Come on," says Jayla,
shooting Alex a look.
"I've got something else for your birthday.
Your mom said you could go with me."
"Where?" I ask.
"I can't tell you. It's a surprise."
We head for the door.
Leave Alex staring at the puzzle on the wall.
The puzzle that is me.
But just when we think we're free and clear,
there's a voice. "Can I come too?"
Alex pulls a tiny prism from his pocket,
rubs his thumb over the glass.
"Please?"
Jayla's fingers curl into fists.
They may be twins,
but she's about to say no
when her mom appears,
drying water droplets off her hands.
"I think that's a great idea."
Jayla stomps out the door.
Alex puts the prism in his pocket,
passes me and asks,
"Where we going?"
I reply, "I don't know.
It's a surprise."
He slowly pulls his eyes
away from the ceiling
so he can look at me,
the way I know he practices.
"I like surprises."

SIRENS AND REFLECTORS

It's not my first time
biking with Alex.
So I'm used to the way he checks his reflectors
for the perfect angle.
Jayla rolls her eyes.
"It's not even dark."
But Alex isn't listening.
We keep to the sidewalks,
Alex on the inside,
because he sometimes gets distracted
and veers toward the street.
Our breath is coming fast
in gasps
as we bike past
houses and shops.
Take the longer way to avoid
the busier—noisier—streets.
"Almost there," says Jayla
over her shoulder.
And right then
is when
the sirens start.
They're headed our way.
Cars
slow to a stop,
and a big, red fire engine
barrels down the street.
I watch,
hold my breath,
make sure it doesn't turn the corner
that leads to my home.

Alex's bike clatters to the ground.
He clamps his hands over his ears,
shakes his head,
backs away.
Quicker than those flashing lights,
Jayla is there,
arm around his shoulders,
reciting color wavelengths.
The only way she can calm him down.

"Yellow:
five eighty.
Orange:
six hundred.
Red:
six thirty."

"Nanometers.
Nanometers.
Nanometers."

SURPRISE

It's the farthest I've ever been allowed to go before.
Ten blocks through the city.
Past tall buildings,
old churches,
staying on the sidewalk
or taking the bike paths
as we glide farther and farther
from home.
I'm twelve now.
And I guess twelve comes with privileges
like this.
Which means Mom would *have* to be
okay
with me continuing baseball season.
I make my plan
as the summer sun beats on my helmet
and sweat runs down my back.
When I see it,
I realize what the surprise is.
I whoop and holler.

The ice-cream shack.

REFUTED

"You shouldn't worry too much,"
says Alex,
licking blue ice cream
from the dark creases of his knuckles.
"Some scientists think Schrödinger's theory,
you know,
about the cat.
The cat I was telling you about."
Jayla sighs. "We know!"
Another slurp,
and Alex goes on.
"Some scientists think it's wrong.
I mean, not very many.
Most scientists agree with it.
But if it makes you feel better
to go against scientific principle
then maybe . . ."
His voice trails off
as he searches for the right thing to say,
and he gets lost in his thoughts.
"Then maybe you should stop talking about it,"
Jayla replies.
Alex lowers his eyes.
I stare at my shoes,
never knowing what to do
when Jayla gets like this.
Her family doesn't wear
paper smiles
like mine.
Everything is real.

"It's okay," I whisper.
"No. It's not," she whispers back.
"It's not okay.
Why does everybody keep saying
it's okay?"
I wiggle my toes,
lick my cone,
keep my mouth closed.

Change the subject.
"Do you guys want to ride with me to baseball?"

"You're not quitting?" asks Jayla.

I take another lick.
"Not a chance."

PRACTICE

Stepping onto the diamond feels like
breathing again
after a long time underwater.
The red dirt belongs
under my feet.
"Cass," Coach yells.
"What are you doing here?
Your mom said you were done for the season."
He jogs over,
puts a hand on my shoulder.
"Sorry about your dad."
I shrug.
"It's okay.
He'll be okay.
But I . . ."

But I what?
I won't be?
Maybe?

"I just need to keep playing baseball."

Coach smiles.
"That I can help with.
Everybody take positions!"

I run to my spot on first base
and field the pop flies, grounders,
and foul balls that
Coach hits my way.

"Hey, Cass!" comes a familiar voice
when I step onto home plate,
swinging my bat
side   to   side.
It's Jack.
Pitcher.
He pulls on the brim
of his yellow Bees hat,
and I wait.
Not for the pitch
but something even better.

TRASH TALK

"Try to hit this one hard.
Your last hit was so soft,
my grandma cut it into pieces,
shoved it in a pillow,
and made a stupid commercial about it."

I'd laugh,
but this is baseball,
and you're not supposed to laugh.
You're supposed to give it back.

Like playing catch
with words.

"Hey, Jack," I reply,
tightening my grip on the bat.
"Try making this pitch fast.
Your last pitch was so slow
I decided to have a tea party with *my* grandma
before hitting it."

"Yeah, yeah," says Jack.
"But go easy on Maxwell.
You know that outfield's
a little too long for his legs."

"Hey!" shouts Max from behind Jack,
but he's not actually mad.
He's the shortest kid on the team,

and we've all got something
we joke about.
That's part of being on a team.

But only *we* get to do the teasing.

Last month, we were playing
the Diamondbacks.
Their pitcher waved everyone forward
when I got up to bat.
He laughed
and thought he was so funny
when he said,
"I got a feeling this one hits like a girl!"

You should have heard the way
my team
yelled from the dugout.
And loudest was Jack.
"Hey! Only I get to say that!"

Finally Jack lets the ball fly
straight toward me—
it curves to the right just slightly,
and I

                                        swing.

MY THIRD WORLD SERIES

I snuck up close to the wall,
leaned way over,
right up close to the dugout
as the players filed in and out.
Ball in one hand,
pen in the other,
reaching,
reaching,
reaching.
Some of the players were nice,
stopping and signing everything.
But there was one
who walked right past
like he didn't even notice me
calling,
asking,
begging.
"Maybe he didn't hear," said Mom.
"No," said Dad. "He heard. He just didn't care."

SANITIZE

The minute I walk in the door,
Mom's already shouting,
"Wash your hands!"
She's on her knees
polishing the baseboards.
I smell bleach.
"Dad hasn't even started chemo yet," I complain.

"He starts soon enough."

The whole apartment is wiped
so crazy clean
it's like something from a magazine.
A picture.
Beautiful but flat.
Lifeless.
I'd like to bend it at the corners,
fold it into something living,
breathing.

But Mom would probably try to scrub away
the creases.

WHERE HAVE YOU BEEN?

"Where have you been?"
Mom asks.
"Oh. Jayla's."
She looks at the clock.
"It's awfully late."
I think about the glove
and cleats
in my backpack that
I just threw in the closet
before she walked in.
Then about how Mom
looked at me today
and lied.
So instead of saying
sorry,
I reply with,
"Oops."
Mom shakes her hands dry.
They're red—
raw.
"Oops?
Cass, I was worried."
Another lie.
Probably.
"I called," she said.
That is true.
She called four times.
"I missed them."
Now I'm the liar.

"I was riding my bike."
Mom frowns. Like she doesn't
believe me. I hold my breath.
"Next time call if you're going to be late,
okay?"
I shrug.
"Yeah, whatever."
Mom looks at me funny.
"Excuse me?"
My whole body feels like
it's been rubbed by a balloon
primed for an electric shock.
I never talk this way to Mom.
I prepare
for a lightning bolt,
but instead
Mom just sighs.
"Come on.
Time for cake."

CAKE AND PRESENTS

It's a cancer year.
A cancer birthday.
Which means smaller,
cheaper,
quieter.
Because soon Dad won't write his articles.
Mom will cut back on her teaching.
My "cake"
is a pan of homemade brownies
warm from the oven,
still gooey and good.
The surprise ingredient?
Peanut-butter chips.
My presents are
a bottle of nail polish,
a stack of rainbow kite paper,
and a poem Dad wrote
just for me.
I smile as I open the presents,
but nothing reaches my heart—
stretches across the icy sea
that separates Mom,
Dad,
and me.
Nothing clears away the secrets
seeping into the spaces between us.
I grip the nail polish in my hand,
feel the smooth curve of the glass,

the one real thing in this whole night
of pretending that everything is okay
and we're being honest with each other.
Then Mom begins
my favorite tradition,
but I can't even look at her
or enjoy it.

THE DAY YOU WERE BORN

"I remember the day you were born.
I'd just finished teaching,
only two days into summer vacation.
I was huge."
"You were not," says Dad.
"I was huge," Mom whispers. "Huge.
I was watering the flowers
out on the balcony.
Just like the flowers we have out there
now.
Marigolds.
Tulips.
Pansies."
My favorite. That's what I'm supposed to say.
What I always say.
But I don't.
Just put the nail polish back on the counter.
"Your favorite," says Mom.
She goes on.
"Then I felt a pop,
and I knew it was time.
I called your dad."
"That was when I worked
at the newspaper," he says.
"Yes. And he rushed home and drove me
right up the hill to the hospital."
"And there wasn't a single bed," I mumble.

I know this story by heart,
but saying it today feels like
taking something sacred
and rolling it in the mud.
Mom acts as if she doesn't notice.
"No! Not one.
I almost had you in the hallway.
And when I held you for the first time—"
"You were perfect," says Dad.
"Perfect," Mom repeats.

MAYBE NOT QUITE PERFECT

"And you still are.
The best thing we ever made."
She reaches out,
runs her hands through
my long, brown waves,
but I pull away.
Her face flashes hurt for a moment,
but still she continues.
"You got my brown eyes,
my long torso,
and my cleft chin.
You got Dad's smile,
his height,
his creativity,
and—"

"*Stop*,"
says Dad.
"Stop.
I can't do this right now."

GUILT

I can see it in his face.
The way he looks at me
like he broke me,
ruined me,
gave me a death sentence.
I can hear it in Mom's voice.
The way she whispers to Dad
as I pick up my presents
and retreat to my room.
"Now is not the time, Sean.
It's not the right time for this."

But I think it is.
So I leave my door open.

EMAIL FROM JAZZ

i will bring u brownies 2 elena.
zucchini brownies. hahaha.

Elena's reply
is there, as well.
I hate you.

WHAT WOULD YOU DO?

I lie on my bed,
stare at the ceiling,
wait for Mom or Dad to come
and pop this bubble forming around me.
This bubble of secrets
and futures
and tests.
Come tell me it will be okay.
But they don't.
Because they don't know that I know.
And I won't tell them.
I finally roll over,
pull out my phone,
and text Jayla.

    What would you do if you were me?
    Would you get the test?

It takes her a few minutes
to respond.
I think so.
My fingers fly.

    Why? Wouldn't you be scared of the answer?

She texts back.
If I were going on a trip
and there were going to be delays,
or gross hotels,
or closed attractions,
I'd want to know ahead of time.
I'd want to make a plan.

MAKE A PLAN

That's it.
If Mom and Dad won't tell me,
won't come to me with this question,
and leave me floating here alone,
then I'll just have to ask it—and answer it—
myself.
I know how to do it.
Research.
Read.
Think critically.
I go to my desk,
turn on the computer,
pull the pamphlet with elephants
from my backpack.
It will be an easy place to start.
I open it
and begin to read.

ELEPHANTS

Elephants have twenty copies
of the p53 gene.
The pictures show the gene as a knight
fighting a cancer dragon.
It's this gene
that closes the windows
and locks the doors
to keep cancer
away.
Humans have only one set of the gene.
I may have none.
None that actually work.
The pamphlet says that maybe one day,
what we learn from elephants about cancer
will save people like Dad—
and maybe me.

The doctor studying this
works right at Hope Circle.
He uses the elephants at the zoo in town.

The zoo where Jayla's dad works
as a vet.

I grab my phone
and text Jayla again.
    Let's go see the elephants tomorrow.

Okay.

SCRIPTURE STUDY

That night when it's time to read scriptures
and pray,
Dad doesn't join us.
"Dad," I call.
But Mom pats my knee
and shakes her head.
"He's too mad right now," she says.
"Mad?" I ask.
"Mad at who?"
But when we begin our prayer—
Dear Heavenly Father—
I think I figure it out.

CALENDAR

Mom follows Dad to their room.
I can hear them
arguing.
This apartment is too small.
The air is clogged with secrets.
I can't breathe.

There's a calendar on the kitchen wall
with pictures of baseball stadiums.
We get it every year.
There's a heart on today.
My birthday.
A heart on
Mom and Dad's anniversary too.
I count the weeks
of Dad's rotating chemo schedule.
Five days in the hospital,
two days at home.
Five days in the hospital,
two weeks at home.
Then do it again,
and again,
and again.
I find the last day
and put a heart on it.
The middle of September.
Six weeks before the World Series.

And just like that,
fresh air.
I still have something to look forward to.

MY SECOND WORLD SERIES

The home team won.
Not just the game, but the whole thing.
Colorful paper squares—
confetti—
burst into the air.
The stadium shook.
The crowd sounded like
a thousand lions.
My eyes were heavy,
and the moon had come out hours before.
As Dad carried me,
he whispered, "Wake up, Cass.
You don't want to miss this."

There's something
almost like electricity
when thousands of people are happy
about the same thing.

They were dancing in the street,
kissing,
singing,
shouting,
and everyone was friends
for just that moment.

PAPER FAMILY

Before bed,
I pull out my scissors
and a piece of thick
red
construction paper.
Then I take white paper—
    fold   snip
        fold   snip.
Cut out the curve of heads,
shoulders,
hands connected,
feet melting
into the white ground.
Glue it into
the red card.
Open it
and a family pops out.
I run my fingers along
the edges of Dad,
Mom,
me,
and wonder
if we're as fragile
as this paper family.
I draw smiles,
paper smiles,
on all their tiny faces.
And put a little extra tape
around the tiny paper hands,
just in case.

TEXT FROM JAYLA

Should we meet in Senegal tonight?
At first I write,
> Sure.

But then I delete it
and write,
> Don't you think we should plan to go to these
> places for real?

I wait a few seconds.
We will!
When we turn eighteen.
Remember?
The next text hurts to type.
> What if I don't have that long?

The reply comes quickly.
Cass. Don't be silly.

> I'm serious.
> The pamphlet said a fifty percent chance of cancer
> by age thirty.
> Eighteen is more than halfway to thirty.
> What if I'm already sick?

What if you don't have the gene at all?
I pause.
> Then Senegal sounds nice.

A minute later, my phone buzzes.
Maybe we should go to Turkey first.
The Pamukkale hot springs
supposedly heal people.

Warmth runs from my fingertips
to my chest,
knowing Jayla
understands,
cares,
knows my secrets.

I smile.
    Turkey?
I text back.
    Now I'm Hungary.
I'm Syrias. Jayla writes.

A giggle rings through my room.
    I know. It's a good plan. Thanks.

GROUP THERAPY 1

My first session back at group therapy.
Elena and Jazz greet me like royalty.
Elena plays a pretend trumpet
when I enter the room.
Jazz announces me.
"You may have thought you'd seen
the last of her genius,
her origami,
her baseball stories—
but ladies and gentlemen,
she just missed us too much.
Let's welcome back
Cassandra Marie Hollens!"
Elena makes crowd-cheering noises.
The rest of the kids in the room
clap awkwardly.
Jazz takes me by the arm.
"Don't mind the newbies.
They've only been here a few months."
Elena sits next to us.
"They still think they're here to talk about
their feelings."
She puts *feelings*
in air quotes.
The counselor, Ms. Holmes,
tells everyone to sit,
introduces me, and says,
"Cass is new to
most
people here."

She looks at our small group—
we call ourselves
the lifers—
as if to tell us to
behave.
We won't,
of course.
Where's the fun in that?
"I'm sure she has a lot of
wisdom
to share with many of you."
Jazz rolls her eyes.
Elena whispers, "Yeah, right."
I wish Blaine were here too.
It's not quite right
without him.
Where is he?

ON WEDNESDAYS

Mom teaches a class online.
Dad writes freelance articles
as much as he can now,
before the chemo knocks him flat.
I go with Jayla to the zoo
where her dad works.
He calls it
zoology-
biology-
geography-
social-science-
volunteering
class.
I call it
the best day of the week.
We go behind the scenes
to see the zoo from the caretaking side,
help feed the animals,
clean cages,
and ask questions.
Lots of questions.
That's the class part.
Then we go home with even more
questions
to look up on our computers
and bring back more the next week.
So when Jayla rings the bell to our apartment,
I bound out of my room
and through the door.
Because Wednesdays
are the best day of the week.

MEERKATS

Jayla's dad meets us by the sno-cone stand.
"I heard you had a request, Cass."
I nod.
"Well, I've got a few animals to check on first.
Okay?"
I shrug.
"Okay."
We follow him to the meerkat enclosure,
where a woman is holding a stack of
red containers. Her hand is on the secret door.
"You taking over feeding today?"
she asks us with a smile.
"If that's okay with you, Jen,"
Mr. Jasper says in his soft, strong voice.
"Be my guest!"
She hands me and Jayla each a container.
"It's snails and grasshoppers today."
I wrinkle my nose. Yuck.
But Jayla lights up. "Cool!"
Inside the enclosure,
a dozen tiny heads
pop   up
      and
                  down
         out
      and   in
of their little holes.
Jayla and I
carefully
pry the lids off our containers
and start

s c   att   e   rin   g
creepy crawlies all around the dirt.
Jayla got grasshoppers.
Lucky.
Half of them
jump
without her having to do anything.
But I have snails
that stick to the container's sides
and slime my hands.
Good thing I'm wearing gloves.
Plop.
Plop.
Plop.
Each of the snails goes to a different corner.
"This is so gross," I say.
Jayla giggles,
turning her already-empty container
upside down.
"Better get used to it,
in case we ever go to France.
They call snails
es . . .
car . . .
go."

"It's what I call
es . . .
car . . .
no."
Jayla snorts.

MEERKATS SAY HELLO

The meerkats emerge—
they know food is here.
They aren't scared of people in their enclosure.
They're used to it.
They put their paws on our boots,
look up
like they're saying,
Wanna play?
Except all they know how to play
is tag,
and you'll never,   ever
catch them.
At least, not without a treat.
I crouch down,
hold out a nasty snail
and wait.
So still,
so calm,
until the smallest one—
Pippin—
scurries up,
snatches it away from me,
and runs back to his burrow.
He pops his head back up,
watching me while he eats.
"Don't worry," I say,
rolling my eyes.
"It's all yours."
There are some delicacies
I don't feel too bad
about missing.

ELEPHANTS

After Jayla's dad
checks out the meerkat named
Frodo,
who has a limp,
he says, "Okay, girls.
Follow me."
He leads us to the far end of the zoo,
through a locked gate,
up behind a building.
There are cement pillars
with thick wire strung between.
On the other side,

elephants.

I step forward,
catch my breath.
"Elephants have twenty sets of the cancer-fighting
p53 gene,"
I whisper.
"I know," says Jayla's dad.
He says it quietly,
not like a whisper,
but like a Sunday-morning prayer
at church.
"This is Hazel.
They're taking a blood sample from her today
to send to the cancer center.
Want to watch?"

I nod and walk to the fence,
feel the metal push into my fingers.
A man gives a signal
and Hazel holds still,
flaps out her ears,
and waits
while they push a tube into an attachment
on her ear
and it fills with blood.

WOOZY

Some people feel woozy
when they see blood.
Some people faint.
But I've seen my dad with an IV
so many times,
it doesn't bother me anymore.
When I see that vial now
full of deep red,
I feel something else.
Grateful.
And I wonder
if it hurts
every time they take a little piece of Hazel.

WANT TO TRY?

"You want to try?"
asks Jayla's dad.
"To take blood?" Jayla squeaks.
She may like grasshoppers
but she doesn't like blood.
He laughs. "No.
Giving Hazel a sign."

He shows us how to raise our hand
and then clench it in a fist
to make Hazel raise her foot.
Jayla tries first.
Hand up,
clenched fist.
But Hazel just stands there
like she doesn't even see Jayla.
"She can be a stubborn one,"
says Mik, the woman in charge of the elephants.
"Don't take it personally."
Then it's my turn.
I take a deep breath,
and stand very still
until Hazel's eyes meet mine.
Hand up,
fist clenched.
Hazel waits—
one second,
two seconds,
three seconds,
before lifting a front foot up off the ground.

"Hey, I think she's taking a shine to you."
Jayla nudges me with her elbow. "Lucky."
Most people
never say that about me.
I don't take my eyes
off of Hazel.

ELEPHANT EYE

Hazel's eyes are golden-orange,
like a sunset in a forest fire.
Eyelashes long and crimped.
Her stare crackles,
burns,
sparks,
as if she's saying,
"I always had the answers.
I was just waiting for you
to ask."
Finally Mik
jolts me back
with a bucket of fruit and carrots.
"Here. She'll love you forever now."

Hazel's trunk sneaks under a wire
when I hold out an apple slice.
Curls around it,
hairy,
like it's covered in short pieces of hay.
Tickling.

I reach out,
pat her trunk,
give her another piece of fruit.
It feels like the only way
to say
thanks.

WHILE JAYLA LEARNS

Jayla learns
about the ivory trade
and looks up more about what it says
on a nearby poster:
ninety-six elephants are killed each day
for their tusks.
I sit on a bench
and lay my hand on the cover
of the elephant pamphlet.
I read the words again,
gently
searching,
as if they are scripture.
I read
about the man studying DNA,
about the drug trials
in five years.
And I wonder
if I could be a part of it.

And even more important,
if it could one day
maybe
help save my dad.
Or me.

LIBRARY

We stop at the library on our way home.
There are kids my age there
using the computers.
I wonder if they realize
how many germs grow on those keyboards.
I ask the librarian for books about
genes.
She gives me
Gregor Mendel: The Friar Who Grew Peas,
The Violinist's Thumb,
and *The Sisterhood of the Traveling Pants*.
"Not those kind of jeans."
The librarian smiles,
winks.
I keep it anyway
and check out *Strictly No Elephants* too.
Just because.

PROS AND CONS OF GETTING TESTED

Pros
1. It might be good news.
2. I could be part of the elephant study.

Cons
1. It might be bad news.

MY EIGHTH WORLD SERIES

The home team was losing.
Five long innings,
not a single run.
The man next to us took off his hat,
turned it inside out,
and wore it to the side.
He told his son
to do the same.
The people on our left,
below us,
above us,
all did it too.
"Rally cap," Dad whispered.
"We'd better follow suit."
"Why?" I asked,
putting my inside-out hat
back on my head.
"To help the team make a comeback."

It seemed silly
until they won,
scoring seven home runs
in the bottom of the ninth,
surprising everyone.

"How did that work?"
Dad kissed my hat hair.
"Hope is a powerful thing."

EMAIL TO ELENA AND JAZZ

Either of you heard
anything from Blaine?
He hasn't emailed me back
yet.

THE MISSING PAMPHLET

When I get home,
I go straight to my room.
To my computer,
my research.
I pull out my pros-and-cons list again,
still pathetically short.
Tap my pencil on the desk.
Where should I start?
I reach for the gray-and-green pamphlet from
yesterday,
the one that laid Dad's life—
my life—
out in numbers.

But it's gone.

Down to the floor I go,
hands and knees,
searching.
A voice from the doorway says,
"Looking for this?"

It's Dad
holding the pamphlet,
a sad smile on his face.
"How much of this have you read?"

I stand,
shrug.
"Most of it."

Dad nods,
sighs,
sits on my bed.
"How much did you understand?"
I fold my arms.
"Most of it."

"So you know."

WHAT I KNOW

The sun rises in the east.
There are fifty states in the USA.
Ostriches cannot fly.
A platypus lays eggs.
Two plus two is four.
My dad has cancer
and a mutated gene
that gets passed along
half of the time.
I am his daughter,
and we are unlucky.

THAT'S WHAT I WAS AFRAID OF

"That's what I was afraid of."
He leans back against the wall,
smacks the pamphlet against his other hand
and waits
for me to say more.
Dad always waits for me to say something.
He doesn't try to fill silence
or move on to other topics.
He understands that some ideas
have to roll around your brain,
pick up speed,
get a bit more polished
before they can come out of your mouth
exactly the way they should.
But the one thought in my brain
that has been there since yesterday
plops out
like a pebble
falling into a lake.
"Why didn't you tell me?"

DAD'S EXCUSE

Dad takes my hand,
then my arm,
and pulls me close to him.
He's strong now.
I try not to think of how weak he'll be soon.
"I wanted to,
but your mom . . .
she thought it was too much,
too heavy,
to place on these shoulders of yours."
He squeezes my shoulders
when he says it.
"She's wrong," I say.
"I'm twelve now."
Dad smiles.
"Ah, yes.
A man loves the meat in his youth
that he cannot endure in his age."
I know it's Shakespeare.
It's always Shakespeare with Dad.
But I don't understand it.
"What does that mean?"
He looks to the ceiling
as if it will give him answers.
"It means some things
are easier to handle,
to think about,
to address,
when you're younger.

Before old age,
melancholy,
and seeing too much of the world
set in."

I ask him *the* question,
my question,
about the test,
but I already know what he'll say.

"I can't answer that for you.
You're twelve.
You can decide for yourself."

It would have been easier
to just be obedient
and do as I'm told.
Maybe Dad is right
and it's better to be young
than old.

DON'T TELL MOM

"Don't tell Mom," I say
as Dad leaves my room.
He stops.
"About this?
Or about the fact that
you're still playing baseball?"
I wince.
"Both.
It's just
with this cancer thing
I'm not ready to . . ."
The words trail off,
but Dad understands.
"You're not ready to hear
Mom's positive side of it?"
I nod.
"That's because there isn't one, Cass.
There isn't one."

PROS AND CONS OF GETTING TESTED

Pros
1. It might be good news.
2. I could be part of the elephant study.

Cons
1. It might be bad news.
2. There is nothing positive about having the gene.

BATTING PRACTICE

"You know what I feel like?" asks Dad.
"Batting practice."
So we walk
across the street
to the diamond and field.
Not the one I practice on,
but any diamond is good.
I step up to the plate,
feel my feet
sink
into the dusty red dirt.
Bang my bat against home plate,
feel the way it gives a tiny bit.
Wrap my fingers around the metal.
Bend my knees.
Elbows out.
Eye on the ball.
Dad throws.
I swing and

CRACK!

"It's going!" Dad shouts
as I run for first base.
"Going!
Gone!"
I do a cartwheel into home
just because I can.

LESS TRAVELED

Another night.
Another poem.
Dad leans on his elbow,
sighs.
"Cass, I picked out a special one tonight.
By Robert Frost.
We've read it before,
but I think you might
hear it differently now."

He reads,
"'Two roads diverged in a yellow wood,
And sorry I could not travel both
And be one traveler, long I stood
And looked down one as far as I could
To where it bent in the undergrowth.'"

I know this poem.
Everyone knows it.
We all know the ending
about two paths
and taking the road less traveled.
But it's the first part that's important.
How long can I stand here
and look down the road?
I can only be one traveler.

HOW LONG DO I HAVE?

"How long do I have?"
I ask Dad as he closes the book.
He coughs.
"What?"
I sigh
and remember
what those words usually mean to a cancer patient.
"How long do I have,"
I say again,
"to decide?
About the test."
Dad leans his cheek on top of my head.
"Life isn't like the library, Cass.
There's no due date.
Whenever you're ready.
But . . .
I can keep it from your mom
for only so long
before it's a breach of trust.
You understand that,
right?"
I do.
But didn't she breach
my trust
first?

WRITE ABOUT THIS

Just as Dad
is about to turn off the light
I ask him,
"You won't write about this,
will you?
You won't write about me on your blog?"
Dad smiles
and sighs.
"This is your life, Cass.
I won't share it with the world
until you're ready.
Or maybe
you can share it
when you're ready."
I think about it
for a second.
"I think I'd like that.
Good night."

"Good night."

EMAIL FROM JAZZ

he wasn't at group last
week. u think he's dead or something?

And Elena wrote back.
Brain hemorrhage from too many
video games probably.

I laugh and type back,
Yeah. Maybe. Hope he still gets
email in heaven.

We joke about death as an
armor. It can't hurt us.

SATURDAY

Jayla meets me
to bike to my game.
Second-to-last one
of the regular season.
I figure if she rides with me,
Mom won't be as mad when she finds out.
If
she finds out.
Plus it makes it less of a lie
when I say
I'm going to hang out with Jayla.
We zip down sidewalks,
around corners,
pointing at imaginary landmarks.
The Arc de Triomphe,
Statue of Liberty,
Taj Mahal.
All the way to the field.
It's a perfect summer evening,
but I can't feel the goodness of it
over the way my stomach
twists
with guilt.

TO BE HEALED

Only one last Sunday
before we start chemo.
Before months of doing church
at home.
Alone.
Which is never quite the same.
The pew is hard.
The bread is stale.
The water is cold.
The speaker stands behind the microphone,
coughs,
begins to talk.
I wave at Jayla
a few rows over.
Fold a paper fan.
But I don't really listen
until a story starts
about a man who takes his sick son
to Jesus.
And Jesus says he can heal the man's son
if the man has faith.
Jesus always says that.
"Faith to be healed."
But the man doesn't have it.
He cries out,
"Help thou mine unbelief!"
I look at Mom.
Tears run down her face.
Dad stares into his hands
like they hold a maze.

And for a moment, I understand Mom.
And the next moment
I understand Dad.

Because it's hard to love God
when he gives you cancer.

But it's hard to hate God
when he also heals.

Destroyer.

Healer.

Which one is he for me?
I take Dad's hand
and say a prayer.
Promise God that I'll have faith enough
for two.

FIRST DAY

First days are important.
First day of school.
First day of summer.
First day of chemo.
I always go with Dad.
There are pictures of me
as a toddler,
holding his hand and walking him
to his very first round
ever,
before I was allowed on the fourth floor
and could only walk him to the front door.
But today is another
first day.
I clutch a book in one hand,
lace my fingers between Dad's
with the other.
Mom grabs Dad's overnight bag
and his other hand.
We all march in together,
Dad bridging the gap that's
growing between

Mom   and   me.

First days are important.
They define how everything else
will go.

This one is no different.

POSITIVE & NEGATIVE SIDES

First day of college,
first day at my first job,
first kiss,
first love,
first day being married,
first day as a mom—
firsts are important.
My future is full
of firsts.

I can't help looking
around
and wondering if this
will be the place
I will also come back to.
So many firsts
I hope to have.
But will they all
be lost
to this one?

MEMORY

The second we get off the elevator,
Dad grabs his stomach,
moans,
throws up in the closest trash can.
Because his body remembers
what's about to happen,
and it's getting ready.

PROS AND CONS OF GETTING TESTED

Pros

1. It might be good news.
2. I could be part of the elephant study.

Cons

1. It might be more bad news.
2. There is nothing positive about having the gene.
3. If I have the gene, I'll feel sick every time
   I think about my future.

CUT OR KILL

There are two ways to get rid of cancer.
Cut
or kill.
If the cancer is small enough—
if it stays locked up tight, without twisting
or working its way
to any other rooms, and
if it hasn't snuck its hand
deep in the cookie jar,
grabbing more and more—
then a scalpel can cut it out,
scrape it away.
Like cancer
never happened.
But if it's escaped—
unlocked the doors
and tiptoed
up

             or

                       down

the stairs, or
had babies and hid them
in cupboards and drawers—
there's only one thing to do.

Kill it.
And everything
around it.

And almost burn down
the entire house in the process.

METHOTREXATE

The bag says *methotrexate*.
A big word,
like something printed
in the list of ingredients
on a cereal box.
But nobody wants to eat this.
The nurses handle the bag with gloves,
special coats,
and masks.
One of them mentions that
she accidentally spilled some
on her arm once.
It left a big,
red
burn.
I wonder if this is why
Dad likes the scripture about the boys
and the fiery furnace
so much.

EMAIL FROM BLAINE

Im here guys. sorry.
my mom is sick. well normal-
people sick. you know.

SAFETY CHECK

Before every practice
and every game,
the boys have to do this thing called
"safety check."

It's the only time I actually feel
weird
being the only girl on the team.

It's like a ritual now.
Coach lines us up
takes us through stretches,
and then
after the last one,
I can see what he's about to say,
and I turn around,
face the other way.
"Safety check!" he calls,
and all the boys laugh and
knock on the hard part of their uniform.
Then I turn back around.
I've decided
it's the boys who are weird.
Not me.

It gives me an idea, though.
And when I pass Jack,
before he can say anything to me,
I say, "Jack,
you're so weird."

Jack smirks,
so I go on.
Just hope he gets it.
Sometimes good jokes
are actually pretty tricky.

"You're so weird,
your mom tried to sell you to a museum,
but they wouldn't accept you.
Didn't think you were real."

Jack opens a piece of gum,
folds it into his mouth.
"Like a platypus?"

I knew I could count on Jack
to understand.

PLATYPUS

Scientists thought platypuses
were a big joke
the first time they saw one.
No animal can be a mammal
and so much like a duck at the same time.
Perhaps I'm a platypus too.
Two different possibilities
combined to make me.

EYE ON THE BALL

At practice
Coach reminds us all to focus.
"Keep your eye on the ball
the whole time.
I don't want your mind thinking about
anything
else."

But all I can see are
everyone's hands
on the grips of the bats.
Everyone's hands
wrapped around the baseballs.
Everyone's hands
touching each other in the huddle.

Hands,
hands,
hands
with germs.

Germs that could kill my dad now that he's in
chemo.

What am I doing here?

WASHING HANDS

It isn't always
cancer
that kills you
when it comes to visit.
Sometimes
when you're burning out
rooms of your house,
trying to get cancer
to leave,
you can't close the door
against other visitors.
Tiny visitors.
Ones with little names
like cold
and flu.
And if your back is turned,
while the fire
is raging,
they'll finish the job of
killing you.

And so,
I carry hand sanitizer
everywhere I go.
Mom scrubs the bathroom,
the kitchen,
the cupboards,
the floor,

and then sits in the corner and cries
because her best friend from college
can no longer come visit
now that she started
coughing.

When I sneak back in from practice,
I scrub my hands—
once,
twice,
three times.

I take off all my clothes
and shower,
scrubbing every inch of skin.

But still I feel the germs
crawling all over me—
itchy,
sharp.

Can't wash away the germs.
Can't wash away the guilt.

EMAIL CHAIN

Email from Jazz:
oh no. is she ok?

Reply from Elena:
Is it the flu?

Email from me:
Are you scared, Blaine?

FIRST CHEMO WEDNESDAY

It's the first Wednesday
during chemo,
and now I'm stuck at home
clicking,
clicking,
clicking on my laptop.
I think of Hazel and
decide to do some research.
One article catches my eye.
It's about how elephants
hear through their feet.
The way they can feel
the language of the Earth
and listen to it move,
rumble,
crack.
I wonder if the separation
of two tectonic plates
feels the way to Hazel
that my mom lying
feels to me.
I wonder if sometimes
Hazel feels the Earth groan
and rip apart
and knows that
everything
is always changing.
That you can't trust
anything.
Not even the ground beneath your feet.

EMAIL FROM BLAINE

To the group:
she's pretty sick. not
in the hospital yet though.
so that's good. I guess.

He emails just me:
yeah. i'm scared.
but please don't tell
Jazz or Elena.

LAST GAME OF THE SEASON

We win.
Well, they win.
I didn't go.
Couldn't go.
Couldn't bear the thought of more germs on my
hands and body
walking through the apartment door with me.
I get a call from Jack.
"We won!
We're going to the playoffs
next week.
Will you be there?"

His voice is full of that shiny
yellow
sound of happiness
and hope.

"I . . . I don't know."

"Come on," says Jack.
"Please? We really need a first baseman
who throws like a girl."

"Edison must have been
good enough," I say.
"Since you still won."

"Edison couldn't catch
a raindrop
even if he was standing in a hurricane."

I laugh.
"And let me guess.
His throws are so short
they got held back in kindergarten."
"Twice!" Jack yells through the phone.

And for a moment
that shiny
hope
is mine too.
"I'll think about it."

"Coach says it's our year.
Our year to win the whole thing."

I hang up the phone
wondering
why I didn't say no.
Why can't I just
say no?

CONCENTRATE

Jayla says I need to concentrate harder
if we're ever going to meet
in our dreams.
She says the problem has to be me
because she imagines a new place for us
so hard every night
she gets a headache.
I know she's right.
It's just hard to concentrate
with the sounds Dad makes in the bathroom
on the other side of the wall
while his body is ridding itself of poison.
But tonight I close my eyes,
block out everything else, and try to
connect our
two souls
across the night.

GUILT IS (PART 1)

Guilt is a snake coiled
in my stomach, ready to
strike at any time.

Like when Mom says, "Cass, thank you
for being so responsible."

Anger is venom.
"Whatever," I spit so I don't
feel bad for lying.

Mom frowns. "I don't think I'm
ready for this teenage stuff."

EMAIL TO BLAINE

I won't tell them.
I promise.

I pause. Unsure what to write next.
I type, It's okay to be scared.
I'm scared too.

But it feels weird
removing my armor.
So I delete that and simply type,
It'll be okay.
Even though I,
out of everyone,
know that can be a lie.

MAYBE

I can't practice.
Can't play in the games.
I know that.
Can't risk the germs
and possibly getting Dad sick.
Nothing is worth that.
Not even the playoffs.
Not even the possibility
of a golden trophy on my shelf
with my name carved into the bottom.
But
maybe
I can still support my team.
Cheer them on.
I won't touch them.
I'll just
watch.
I decide this is an okay plan.
It doesn't really
put Dad at risk,
and it still lets me
be a part of it.
A part of the game.
The win.

THROUGH THE CHAIN LINK

"Guys, it's Cass!" someone shouts,
and they all come running
but stop short when I say,
"Not too close!"
I put my hands in front of me
like I'm about to slide
out of reach.
"What are you doing here?" asks Max.
"Are you gonna play?" shouts Edison.
Jack isn't smiling.
I think he already knows my answer.
"No. Too many germs."
They all moan together.
"But I came to
cheer you on."
They try to act
like that's enough.
Try to smile
as they walk away.
I try to pretend
that I'm okay.

JACK ASKS AGAIN

Jack hangs out by the fence
the longest.

"You sure you can't play?"
"I'm sure. If my dad gets sick . . .
well, he just can't get sick."

Jack nods. "My mom's diabetic.
So . . . I've been there."
I know he's talking about the pandemic
that kept people mostly at home
for weeks or months
and others close to home a lot longer.
"I couldn't play baseball for a while.
I hated it," Jack says. "But my mom's alive."
He shrugs,
without saying the obvious part:
it was worth it.
"Thanks for understanding," I say.
Jack cracks the gum in his mouth.
"Cass, if you're going to cheer for us,
you better be loud."

"How loud?" I ask,
knowing what's coming next.

"You better be so loud
that my grandma will decide
to turn off her hearing aid."

I grin. "Deal."

THERE'S A DIFFERENCE (PART I)

There's a difference
Between standing on the red dirt
playing the game
and standing behind the chain link
watching it.

I yell,
      and yell,
            and yell,
                 and yell,
loud enough to cut through
the cheers of the crowd on the bleachers
who I stay   far away from.

"This next hit's coming for you!"
"Shake it off!"
"You kidding me? That wasn't a strike!"

But that shiny
hope
fades away to something dull
and aching.

I leave during the last inning
when I know we're going to lose.
Can't face everyone's eyes,
knowing that if I'd stepped onto
that diamond today,
maybe things would have been different.
Maybe it would have really been our year.

MOM'S ENERGY

Mom meets me at the door.
"How was Jayla's?"
"Fine," I lie.
Squeezing past her,
not wanting to meet her eyes,
not wanting to see her paper smile,
or hear how great
everything is right now.
Lies.
My mom is nothing
but one big . . .
"I made snickerdoodles."
I pause
and turn to face her.
"You've been so . . .
distant."
Mom twists the ring
on her finger.
"I know you're growing up,
and this is all normal,
but . . .
I miss you.
Could we sit and talk
about something besides
ancient Egypt
or the area of a triangle?"
Or genetics,
cancer whispers in my ear.

Or dying before you're thirty.
Can't talk about that either.
"I'm tired," I say.
And it's not a lie.
Not really.
I'm very, very tired
of all of this.

GUILT IS (PART II)

Guilt is avoiding
phone calls from your coach, teammates
checking in to see
how everything is going.

What they mean is, "It's your fault."

GROUP THERAPY II

Ms. Holmes claps
to get everyone's attention.
"We have a few
new faces today.
So how about we play
a round of
two truths and a lie."
Some of the newbies groan.
"I'm running out of truths!"
one of them complains.
"Sucker," whispers Jazz.
"He obviously doesn't know
how to play it right."

The secret to winning
two truths and a lie
is to tell three lies
and then never,
ever
admit it.
Not only do you win
by never admitting a lie,
but you also win
by never telling anybody
anything true.
An important part
of being a lifer.

When it gets to Elena,
she stands and says,
"Okay. I'm a world champion
sumo wrestler,
I hate chocolate,
and I once sang the national anthem
at a Bees game."

One kid shouts out,
"Sumo wrestling!"
Elena gets these big eyes and says,
"Nope."

Everyone groans.
Even Ms. Holmes.
And Elena sits down with a grin,
having fulfilled her mission.

Next Jazz claims to have killed a wolf
with her bare hands,
hacked the Pentagon's computers,
and saved every booger she's ever picked.

"If the booger thing isn't the lie,
I'm kicking you out," says Ms. Holmes.

"You can't do that!" says Jazz.
But they're both laughing.
Both lying.

I usually love
three lies and no truth.
But today—
I don't know—
I've had enough of lies.
So I try something
a little different.

"Hi everyone,
I'm Cass.
And,
um,
I can talk to elephants—
kind of;
I've been to the World Series
eight times;
and I'm a platypus."

Ms. Holmes laughs.
"You three,
always making this two lies and a truth."

But she's wrong.
All of mine were the truth.

A FEW WEEKS LATER

In early August,
poison keeps flowing down narrow tubes,
running through Dad and sweeping out
all the cancer.
I sit next to him and watch the game.
A pitch, a crack, a pop fly.
"Easy out," says Dad.
But it isn't always.
Because balls can be dropped.
I've done it before.
And for all the time the ball is flying,
the batter is a bit like me.
Like Schrödinger's cat.
Both safe and out
at the same time
until the ball lands in glove or grass,
and he knows.
Knows for sure.

THE GAME

"You think we'll see the Cubs at the Series
this year?" Dad asks.

> I don't.

"I can't wait to go. Maybe we'll catch
a home-run ball."

> I hope.

Dad's new doctor takes off his glasses
and clears his throat.

> I wait.

"You're not really planning on going to
the World Series this year, are you?"

> I am.

"As your doctor, I have to advise
against it. Your immune system can't
handle the stress."

> I freeze.

Dad pats my hand. "We're supposed
to be done by then."

> I breathe.

"You've been doing so well.
We're extending your treatment.
Two more rounds, just to be safe."

> I count.

"That means I'll still be here in November.
Not much of a reward," Dad jokes.

> I laugh.

"I'm sorry," says the doctor. "It's just
not possible. You can't go."

> I hate.

CANCER CHANGES THINGS

Why does my world keep
shattering
with just a few words?

After the doctor—
Dr. Barry—
leaves,
Dad turns to me and says,
"I'm sorry.
He didn't need to break that news
in front of you."
"Is it true?" I ask.
He looks right at me.
"My chemo's never
intersected
with the Series before.
But he's the doctor. He's probably right."
Dad sighs as Mom walks into the room.
"What's wrong?" she asks.
"We can't go to the World Series," says Dad.
I don't say anything.
Mom tries to pull me close,
but I stop her.
"It's not fair," I whisper. "It's not fair."
"We go to the World Series every year,"
says Mom. "I think we can miss one time."
"No.
It's not supposed to be like this.
It's not supposed to change!"
"I know. I'm sorry. But Cass," Dad whispers.
"Cancer changes everything."

EVERYTHING

The moon revolves around the earth
every 27.3 days.
The earth revolves around the sun
every 365.3 days.
Spring, summer, fall, winter.
Flowers bloom, leaves fall.
Cancer doesn't change
everything.
And every year,
the World Series happens.

THERE'S A DIFFERENCE (PART II)

"We can still watch the Series on TV," Mom says.
"I'll make nachos and hot dogs.
It will be . . .
it will be, you know, similar."

There's a difference
between watching the game
from a hard seat
in a crowd of thousands,
and watching the game
from a soft couch
with just three people.

I don't say anything, though.
Mom already knows.

PROS AND CONS OF GETTING TESTED

Pros
1. It might be good news.
2. I can be part of the elephant study.
3. I will know to do as much as I can and live
   as much as I can now, before I get sick.

Cons
1. It might be more bad news.
2. There's nothing positive about having the gene.
3. If I have the gene, I'll feel sick every time
   I think about my future.

MY FIRST WORLD SERIES

Dad got to throw
the opening pitch.
His blog had gone viral
a couple months before.
I don't remember much.
I was only four.
But I remember standing on the side of the field.
I remember the thunder of the stadium.

I know now that people called him an inspiration,
and said his words made them
stop—
consider their priorities.

But I didn't know that then.
All I knew was that right
before he strode onto that field,
Mom whispered,
"Are you nervous?"
Dad grinned,
his head barely covered
in a thin layer of fuzz.
"I might die of fright."
Mom laughed,
smacked his butt as he walked away.
"Go get 'em."

SOLUTION

As soon as we get home from the doctor,
I unlock my bike from the rack.
"Please stay here," says Mom.
"We can play a game.
Something to cheer us up."

But I can't.
Because I have a problem without an answer.
And when that happens,
I have to go
to the smartest person I know.
The only person who can figure out any
solution.

And this time,
when I say I'm going to Jayla's house,
it's actually the truth.

LOOKING FOR SOMEONE ELSE

When Jayla opens the door,
she smiles and flips
her new spiral braids,
like she's been expecting me,
even though I know I'm interrupting dinner.
Her mom is right behind her.
"Cass! Wanna eat?"
I shake my head,
and peek behind them both.
        "Is Alex home?"
Jayla looks at me like I asked to lick a frog.
"You want to talk to Alex?"
        "I have a problem."
"That Alex can solve?"
        "I hope so."

TO THE POINT

You don't tell stories
to Alex.
You don't start with a joke,
beat around the bush,
or talk around a problem.
You say what you mean,
and you say it exactly,
or he stops listening.
Or he doesn't understand.
Or he looks at you like you
are the dumbest person on the planet.
So I state my problem like
an experiment,
and pray
as he gets
to work.

PERFECT STORM

Words swirl around and around in the air like
they're caught in updrafts of wind and thrown
around with no particular care about where they'll
land or how they'll feel to those listening.
Words like *immunocompromised, death, antiseptic,*
antigen, antibiotics,
sanitized, contagion, germ, biological warfare, viral,
communicable disease, hands, mouths,
breathing, blood, bodily fluids,
mask, gloves, isolation.
All of it condensing
into a single
solution:

private
box
seats.

BOX SEATS

Box seats are for people who want
to watch the game
behind a pane of glass,
eat fancy food, and talk about
fancy cars and fancy houses.
They're for important people—
rich people.
Not for people with a constantly accumulating
hospital bill.
A bill that will never be paid.
Not for people who don't actually buy
their own seats,
but who are at the park because
someone else got the tickets.
It's plain outdoor seats for us.
With cheap hot dogs
and fly balls.
A gift we can never repay.
How will I ever get Dad box seats?
Especially private ones with nobody else around?

I look at Alex.
"It's impossible."

A SQUEEZE

I drop into a chair.
As if the words
box seats
weigh a thousand pounds.
Alex erases something on the board.
"It's not impossible. Simply improbable."
I know he's trying to make me feel better.
But it's like when Mom squeezes my shoulder
and accidentally pinches my collarbone
instead.

Alex has always been
a little confusing.
The way he says things,
does things.
Especially the way
he looks at me lately.
Like I'm a math problem he's trying
to figure out.

Alex isn't that confusing, though,
when you really know him
and give him a chance.
Give him time to take in
all the facts, all the noise,
all the thoughts in his head.
I understand that.

"Thanks, Alex. That's really sweet."
And I mean it.
Alex looks at me like I handed him
a present.
And I have to turn away.

PROUD

Jayla holds her head
higher. Whispers something. Gives
Alex a fist bump.

WHAT ABOUT

"What about a bake sale?"
Jayla asks.
"People like cookies and brownies,
stuff like that."
I nod.
"Maybe."
That's good enough for Jayla.
She marches into the kitchen
and pulls out box
after box
of mixes,
chocolate chips,
flour,
sugar,
sprinkles, and bits.
"My mom always has stuff like this.
You know, food storage.
She says she doesn't want to survive any sort of
apocalypse
without dessert."
I laugh and walk up to the counter.
Alex joins us,
whisk in hand.
"I get to lick the bowl."

SWEET THINGS

It's eight o'clock at night
when we finish baking.
Plates stacked high with
sugared,
chocolatey,
frosted
hope.
"I'll have my mom bring a couple plates by your
house tomorrow," says Jayla
as she runs to the garage to get her bike.
It's time for me to go.
Alex walks me to the door.
"Thanks," I say.
"Thank you!" Alex blurts at the same time.
"For letting me lick the spoon.
It was really good—
I mean sweet.
Well, it was both
because of the sugar.
Sweet and good."
I can't help it—after he closes the door,
I shake my head
and think
about cookies,
and Alex,
and hope.
Sweet things.

BIKING ME HOME

Jayla's long black braids
fly out from behind
and beneath her helmet
as she pedals in front of me.
"You know, in the Netherlands,"
she calls back,
"they ride bikes everywhere."
When she drops me off at my apartment
she adds,
"Maybe that's where we should go."

I think of the money
we're trying to earn
to send
me
to the Series
when all Jayla wants to do
is escape
and travel.
I'm pretty lucky to have her for a friend.
So I say,
"I don't know. I'm back to thinking
Senegal
sounds pretty good."
Jayla beams.

WHEN I GET HOME

Mom's eyes are red
around the edges.
"Where were you?" she whispers.
"At Jayla's."
She has a package of Oreos.
Swirls one in a glass of milk.
"Are you sure?
Sure it wasn't
baseball practice?"
I freeze.
"Oh yes.
I know.
I got to find out today
in the grocery store,
when your coach stopped to tell me
how admirable he thought it was
that you kept playing after
your dad's diagnosis."
She sniffs,
and her Oreo falls apart in the milk,
black bits sinking to the bottom of the cup.
"I can't believe you would be so selfish
to put your dad's life
at risk
like that."

"I didn't—" I try to say.
"It was only once—"

"But what's worse
is that you lied to us about it.
Kept it a secret."

Yeah, I know,
I think.
People keeping secrets is terrible.

And that thought
almost
makes me feel better.
Like I am in the right.
Almost
pacifies the snake in my gut.
Almost
dries up all the guilt.

Mom doesn't come into my room that night
to light my candle.

I'm getting too old for that anyway.

EMAIL TO THE LIFERS

I'm doing a bake sale tomorrow at the hospital.
Think I can get the doctors to buy anything?

Elena says: Forget the doctors!
Sneak it all to me!
I've eaten so much zucchini
my skin is turning green!

Jazz says: they should
with all that moolah they make

Blaine says, just to me:
My mom got worse.
She's there now
with strep.

I write back.
If I see her, I'll give her something.

COLD SHOULDER

Mom doesn't ask for details
when Mrs. Jasper brings the plates of cookies.
I take them in the car
to Hope Circle,
up the elevator
to the fourth floor.
I don't tell her why.
Because we don't talk
at all.
And that's fine.

Really.

SUGAR AND INTERVIEWS

I set up shop
at the nurses' station.
People trade in their quarters,
their coins, and
their cash.
For a tiny bit of sugar.
And that's when I decide to ask
my question.
The question
hanging over my head.
The secret that
Mom won't talk about.
"What would you do
if you were me?
If you could see the future,
would you choose to see?"

I WRITE DOWN THEIR ANSWERS

Yes.

"An ounce of prevention is worth
a pound of cure."

No.

"I've seen too much
of what happens to people
after they get cancer.
I wouldn't want to know that's coming."

No.

"Cancer's tricky.
Even if you catch it early,
doesn't mean you'll survive.
Take the patient I saw today."

Yes.

"There are people in my life
I'd need to prepare.
Make arrangements.
If I knew that was coming."

Yes.

"Seen too many people
not prepared for cancer.
Wouldn't want to be one of 'em."

No.

"I wouldn't choose to live
with a death sentence
hanging over me."

It's all a mess.
So many reasons,
so many whys.
I sell all my cookies,
say goodbye,
and tiptoe down the hall.
I look through every door,
but I don't see Blaine's mom.
She might be on a different floor,
or at a different hospital—
in one of those clean rooms
to keep all the germs
OUT.
I wish she were here, though.
Maybe she'd have
an answer for me.

TEXT TO JAYLA

$48.

She texts back,
$15. My dad ate
a whole plate
last night.
Sorry.

It doesn't take a math genius
to figure out what to write next.

I don't think this will work.

Maybe not. 🙁

I try to put on a paper smile.
Try to text,
   At least we tried, right?
But my fingers slip.
They won't press send,
and I end
up
screaming into my pillow instead.

FAMILY TREE

My dad's adopted.
The oncologist said we might have
known
about his gene earlier
if he weren't.
His mom and dad were older
when they brought him home.
They're gone now.
Dad says he's glad they don't have to see him
like this.
But I don't believe him.
Mom is the youngest of three.
Her mom lives in Arizona
where she takes care of my grandpa,
who doesn't remember me
anymore.
Mom's two sisters live on the East Coast
with babies galore.
So they can't come and help,
but they call every day.
When I answer the phone,
their voices catch.
"Cass—
how you doing, sweetie?"
And I know
they know
about me.
Something inside
boils up.

At them for knowing,
for feeling bad for me.
At Mom for knowing,
knowing,
knowing.
Telling everyone but me.
I won't talk to her—
or them—
about genes
or decisions.
So I say, "The Mets bullpen
looks strong this year.
Maybe we'll get to see you guys
when we go to the World Series."
They always say,
"That would be wonderful!"

But I don't believe them.

GROUP THERAPY III

Before we get started,
Elena walks in rubbing her eyes.
They're red and teary.
She sneezes.
Jazz and I both scoot our chairs
back
at least three feet.
"Uh, are you sick?" asks Jazz.
"You know you're not supposed to be here
if you're sick."
Elena wipes away another tear.
"Not sick. It's just allergies."
Jazz whips out her phone.
"*Mmmhmm*. What are your
symptoms?"
Elena sighs.
"Watery eyes,
sneezing,
itchy ears."
Jazz types it in,
then sucks in her breath.
"Oooh. Bad news."
The corner of her lip
twitches up.
"You probably have cancer."
We don't stop laughing
until Ms. Holmes tells us to
settle down
at least three times.

EMAIL TO BLAINE

Missed you at group today.
How's your mom?

He writes back.
She's getting
better. I think.
Hopefully, she'll be back home soon.
My dad seems to miss cleaning up puke.
Because he keeps feeding us
Spam and broccoli.

I write back:
Gross. haha

THE HOUSE OF MOURNING

"You know, not all the tombs
in Egypt are for pharaohs,"
Mom says to me one day
during school time.
"Take a look at this one.
The inscription says,
'sole friend of the king'
and 'keeper of the secret
of the Morning House.'
That's the place
where the pharaoh had breakfast
and got dressed."
Mom laughs.
"It sort of feels like the kind of thing
that will be written on my headstone
one day.
What do you think?"
I tap my pencil
on my notebook
and decide to poke Mom
and see what she says.
Give her a chance
to make things right.
"What's the secret you keep?" I ask.
"*My* secret . . ."
She leans forward
over the table.
And for a moment I think
this is it—

we can close the gap
and come back together.
But Mom doesn't notice—
or doesn't realize—
what I'm really asking.
"Is that waffles are
the superior breakfast food."
Mom laughs,
feeding me
stale jokes
when I am starving for
the truth.

MIDDLES

Middles aren't important
or exciting
or particularly good
for anything.
At least, that's what you'd think
from the way people talk about them.
Middle of nowhere,
midlife crisis,
cutting out the middleman.
The middle of chemo is the same way.
You're always in the middle of
hair falling out,
poking back up,
falling out again.
Throw up,
clean up,
throw up,
feel better,
throw up again.
Go to the hospital,
go home,
go back,
go home again.
And when you're in the middle,
you watch the seasons change
from behind closed windows
and locked doors
to keep the germs at bay.
So I watch as the flowering cherry
begins to turn to flame
and summer fades away.

THERE'S A DIFFERENCE (PART III)

There's a difference
between living life
and watching
everyone else live theirs.

BASEBALL BY YOURSELF

They say baseball's a team sport,
but that doesn't mean you can't play it by yourself.
Because sometimes
it's the best thing
for a brain that won't stop thinking.
So I grab my glove
and bat
and ignore Mom's silence
that says so much
as I head out the door to the field.

First I stand
on the pitcher's mound,
feel the baseball in my hand.
Run my fingers
over
the stitches.
Pull my arm back
and throw.

Then I stand
to the right of home plate.
Toss the ball,
hurry to grip,
then swing.
Retrieve,
throw,
grip,
swing.

It's relaxing.
Like a rhythm.
And in my mind I hear
the crowd
chanting
and the outfield
jeering.

Hey, batter batter.
Hey, batter batter.

Throw,
grip,
SWING!

MISSING IT

Every Sunday
the boys bring the sacrament,
the ladies from church bring a parade of casseroles,
and Sister Rowan brings me papers
about what they learned in Young Women's
and what they're doing for activity that week,
even though Jayla already tells me everything.
I'm missing it.
I'm missing all of it.
And what if I end up missing
my entire life?
Because cancer comes to visit
and never leaves.

MAKEUP TUTORIAL

Jayla got a makeover
from one of the older girls at church.
One day of looking pretty,
and now she wants me to try it.
Makeup,
mascara,
lip gloss.
She comes over
(after swearing up and down
she's not even a little bit sick)
with a big, pink box.
The outside is plastered
in postcards.
All the places Jayla wants to go
one day
when she can get away.
The inside is full
of supplies.
And for just a minute
I feel
young and babyish.
I've never really worn makeup before—
not even sure I want to.
But then Mom walks by and says,
"You girls are too pretty and young
to get started with"—
she waves
—"all of this."
And even though she's smiling,
I can tell it really does
kind of bother her.

Which is all I need to know.
"Okay," I say. "Put it on."
And Jayla does,
carefully,
before giggling
and saying,
"My makeup won't work on you.
It's way too dark."
I look at myself in the mirror,
and laugh at how the plum-colored blush
looks so strange on me
but so good on Jayla.
We creep into the bathroom,
swipe Mom's makeup bag,
and do our best with her limited supply.
Finally Jayla cocks her head and says,
"You're ready."

READY

The words stir inside me.
Ready?
Ready for everything I have to know
and do?
I look in the mirror.
Somebody else stares back at me.
"Whoa," I whisper.
"I know, right?"
On the outside
I look like one of the older girls at church,
the ones who probably know everything.
But on the inside,
I still feel
twelve,
scared,
and not ready.
For anything.

SPANISH PRACTICE

Both Jayla and I have been learning Spanish
ever since second grade.
Supposedly.
Our moms have tried every app
and program they can find.
But none of our parents speak it
so
nothing has really worked.
They keep trying, though.
"Okay, girls." Jayla's mom's voice
echoes
through the laptop.
On my screen I get a look
right up her nose
while she gets our video call working.
"No boogers!" I shout.
"Oops!"
Mrs. Jasper laughs,
and instead of adjusting the screen
like most adults would,
she leans in closer.
"Are you sure?" she says in her best
nasally voice.
"Check it real good now."
"Mooomm," Jayla whines off-screen.
"Stop!"
But I can hear that she's laughing.
Mrs. Jasper cackles
and slides out of the way.
"All right, all right.
You girls practice now.

I want to hear only Spanish
for the next twenty minutes.
Got it?"
We both nod
and giggle
and wave
at the little pictures of each other.
Jayla sticks her tongue out.
I cross my eyes.
Mrs. Jasper pops back in.
"How come I'm not hearing any
hola or
como se LA-ma
or whatever?"
Jayla rolls her eyes.
"*Como se* la-ma, Mom?"
"Yeah!" Mrs. Jasper cackles again.
"Which reminds me.
Alpaca you a lunch
right now!"
Jayla covers her face with her hands.
"Mom, that was terrible."
Mrs. Jasper just laughs some more
and closes the door.

QUESO EN MIS PANTALONES

Jayla and I spend the next twenty minutes
telling each other
about what is in our *pantalones.*
Queso,
tacos,
perros,
libros,
elefantes,
and of course
piernas.

ELEPHANTS AT CLOSING

Jayla's dad sneaks us into the zoo
after closing time.
The only time I can go
these days,
because everybody's gone.
I race to the elephants with
Jayla on my heels.
Hazel is there,
right up against the fence.
"Hi," I whisper.
She blows air out of her trunk
and swings it around.
Jayla wanders over
to the two elephants on the other side.
But I'm not interested
in them.
Jayla's dad hands me
a bucket of fruit.
"Her appetite has gone down lately," he says.
"I'm worried about her.
See how she does with this."
"Are you hungry, Hazel?" I ask.
She opens her mouth
and points to it with her trunk.
"Course you are."
I feed her bit by bit.
Tell her
about my genes,
and her genes,
and how we're connected.
And then I remember.

ELEPHANTS HEAR WITH THEIR FEET

I look down at Hazel's foot,
giant, wide, and flat.
I lift my hand in the air,
clench my fist,
and up goes her foot.
When I lower my fist, her foot goes back down—
STOMP.
I swear I can feel the earth
tremble beneath me
just a little.
Maybe Hazel can't understand my words.
I stomp.
"Hi, Hazel."
I imagine the message traveling through the ground
to Hazel's foot and then her brain.
I stomp again.
"Hi, Hazel."
She watches me, flaps out her ears,
and sneaks her trunk through the wire to try and
snatch
a carrot from my bucket.
I give her one,
then stomp again.
"Hi, Hazel."
This time
without me raising a hand,
she picks up her own foot and
stomps,
stomps,
stomps.
Hi, Cass.

THE CANCER LIBRARY

There is a library in the cancer center.
I've never gone inside before.
It doesn't have the kind of books
I usually like to read.
Everything there is about
nutrition,
clinical trials,
treatments, and
cancer, cancer, cancer.
Who needs to read about it
when you're living it?
But today
I stand in the doorway,
pros-and-cons list
and pamphlet
in my hand.
I have to know more
if I'll ever be able to make this decision
on my own.
All alone.

THE CANCER LIBRARIAN

The library is just one room—
a few bookshelves—
but the librarian here is like all librarians
everywhere.

Helpful,
smiling.

My hands shake
as I give her the pamphlet.
The words get stuck when I say,
"I need to know more
about this."
She flips open the cover,
skims it for a minute,
then smiles.
"I've got just the thing."
She doesn't ask why
I need it,
which is good.
I'm not ready to tell.
But I think
maybe
she already knows,
because of the way her arm wraps
around my shoulders
as she leads me to a corner,
pulls a thick book off the shelf,
and gently puts it in my hands.
p53: The Gene That Cracked the Cancer Code.

It's heavy,
like it holds entire lives inside it.
"No due date," she whispers.
"Whenever you're ready."
And as I stand in the doorway,
I feel cancer beside me,
but I hear Dad's words echo.
Whenever you're ready.

A VOICEMAIL FROM COACH

Hey Cass, we're having
our pizza party today.
Should we bring you some?

A VOICEMAIL FROM JACK

Cass, you should have been
at the party. It was wild!
The cheese on my pizza
was so stretchy, I could have
used it as a belt. So gross!

A VOICEMAIL FROM MAXWELL

Cass, I told my mom I missed seeing you,
and she said I should call and tell you that.
I told her that's not what we do,
and she said that's silly and handed me the phone.
So, um . . . yeah.
Bye.

                    (Are you happy now, Mom?)

BEFORE BED

Dad sits on my bed.
No poems tonight.
Finding a good one takes
energy,
and he doesn't have much of that.

"Have you thought about the test?"
All day
every day—
but that's not what I say.
"A little."

"Do you want to talk about it?"
Yes.
All the time.
His questions feel like a sword
tearing me apart from the inside.

I look at Dad
see his eyes halfway closed,
hear his tired sigh.
Feel cancer take a seat
behind him.
"Not right now."

EMAIL TO BLAINE

Any news? I write.
For a moment, I think about
taking off my armor with him,
and being honest.
Really honest.
Telling him about being
a cat in a box—
dead and alive at the same time.
A platypus—
but I chicken out.

Blaine writes back.
my mom came home today.
she looks really bad
and is sleeping most of the time.
but i know she's feeling a little better, because
my dad cooked Spam
for dinner again tonight, and my mom asked
if he was trying to speed up
her whole dying thing.
we all laughed.
even dad.
my grandma
is here to help mom, and she
didn't think it was very funny though.
anyways
i'm really glad she's home
and not dead.

At first I think,
maybe I can share with him
all the fear inside of me.
Isn't that what he's doing here?
But then he finishes with,
I'd hate to starve to death.
And just like that
Blaine's armor is back on.
I'm glad I didn't tell him
about the dents
in mine.

MY FIFTH WORLD SERIES

You can't
not
do the wave
at the World Series.
Can't be the only person
in a sea of moving bodies
who sinks deeper
into their seat.
It was like everyone—
all the thousands of people
in one stadium—
were pieces
in a giant
Rube Goldberg machine,
and the sole purpose
was making my dad
smile.
He'd been sick so much that year.
I would have done
a thousand waves
to see that smile.
"Are you happy, Daddy?" I asked him
as we both sat down.
He put his arm
around my shoulders.
"I'm always happy with you, kiddo."

ALL AUGUST

When Dad's white blood cell counts are up,
I'm allowed to go
to Jayla's house
and group therapy
only.
Nowhere else is safe
except
the flowering cherry across the street.
So on the good days,
and the bad days,
I sit beneath the tree and watch
kids pass by.
The days march toward fall.
Mom's anger fades away.
She's back to paper smiles.
Like I never lied and kept a secret.
Even though I did,
and she still is.

My collection of paper shapes
grows larger
and larger.
Leaves,
birds,
caterpillars,

and elephants.

I wish
there were real elephants
beneath the flowering cherry.
Wish Hazel could hear my thoughts
through her feet
in this shade.
But I feel her all around me
just the same.
Feel the burning of her
forest-fire sunset eyes.
My questions.
Her answers.

Fold and crinkle,
bend and smooth.
The paper forms something
I didn't expect.

Hope.

ANOTHER WEDNESDAY

We're cleaning out the parrot enclosure
this time. It's always fun,
and today is even more so
because Alex is here.
The parrots like Alex.
He can make them do things
nobody else can.
Say funny things, like
eureka!
And when Alex says,
"Luke"
in his best Darth Vader voice,
one parrot always responds with
"I am your father."
Today, we try something new
that we read about online.
Teaching the parrots
new songs.
So as we sweep
and clean up poop
(which isn't as gross as it sounds,
I swear),
we whistle the Mario Brothers theme music.
Just the beginning.
Over and over.
The birds don't seem to be catching on.
"Maybe we should try
something else,"

Jayla says.
Alex shakes his head
but doesn't look up from the ground he's sweeping.
Sings,
                              dum!"
"Ba   da   da   da
                  ba
And somehow,
like magic
(though Alex would argue
it's purely science),
a parrot sings back:
"Bum   bum
        bum   bum   bum
              bum   bum."
And then Jayla and I
shake our heads.
Because we'll never be
as good at this as Alex.
Never.

A NEW MESSAGE

Jayla's dad takes us to see Hazel again.
As soon as she sees me,
Hazel stomps three times.
"Whoa," says Jayla.
"She remembers."
I stomp three times back.
"That's how we say hello,"
I tell Alex.
He peers at Hazel
the way he sometimes does at me,
like he's trying to figure out
something she's not saying.
"Does she know that?" he asks.
I nod. "I think so."
But today
I want to teach her something new.
So once I'm given a bucket,
I hand Hazel a carrot,
then stomp once—
pause—
pause—
stomp again—
then say,
"Thank you."
Hazel watches
but she doesn't respond.
Jayla and Alex stand behind me
like I'm a magician
who just pulled Hazel from a hat.

I give her another carrot.
Stomp.
Pause,
pause,
stomp.
"Thank you."
I do it again
and again
and again.
Until all the carrots and apples
are gone.
Hazel watches me,
but she doesn't say it back.
"Maybe," says Alex,
"she thinks you're the only one
who needs to say thank you."
And I can't help thinking
he's kind of right.

SOMETHING MORE

Once more before we leave,
I say it again,
and Hazel reaches out her trunk
to touch my face
and snuffle my hair.
Maybe she's just looking for
a few last carrots,
or maybe
it's something more.

JAYLA'S SECOND IDEA

We pass time beneath the cherry tree.
Jayla on her back,
book in hand
blocking out the sun.
"Venice,
Rome,
lasagna.
Don't you think we should go to Italy?"
But I'm not thinking
about leaving.
I'm staring back at my apartment building,
at the window to my parents' room,
thinking of how Dad groaned
and threw up
all night.
So it takes me a little longer
to come up with a reply.
"I'll think about Italy-tle bit."
Jayla snorts,
goes back
to fingering the pages of
cathedrals, basilicas, gondolas.
Dreams.
Then finally she says,
"I've been thinking.
Why don't we ask the people who read your dad's
blog
for help to pay
for private box seats?"
I pull a tuft of grass.

Squeezed stomach,
heart stretched thin,
the fear that I
am wrong
for wanting this.

I can hear the echo of Dad last night.
The way he leaned against the bathroom wall
and cried
when he thought I was sleeping.

But the echo can't drown out my want.
So I nod.
"I'll talk to my mom about it."

ASKING

I wait a day
until Dad is back in treatment,
and Mom and I are eating dinner at home
before visiting the hospital.

"I was thinking,
you know,
about Dad and the World Series."
Cut,
cut,
nod.
"What if we got
private box seats?"
Chew,
chew,
"*Hmmm.*"
She says,
"That's really expensive."
One,
two,
three—
say it.
"Maybe Dad's blog can help."
Breathe in.
Breathe out.
"Maybe
we
can
ask."

NOBODY CARES

I twist my napkin,
fold,
swirl it
into a swan
while I wait for Mom's answer.

"Honey,
the people who read Dad's blog
already ran a big fundraiser for us
back in June when they found out.
You know that.
We can't ask for more."

"But this is different," I say.
"This is for the World Series."

"Cass, they gave us money to live off of.
Nobody cares if we go to the World Series."

I crumple my napkin swan
into a hard little ball.

Mom makes it sound like there's only so much
caring
people can do.
Like you can run out of it.
But that doesn't seem right to me.

"You're the one who doesn't care."

I CARE

Mom scoots back in her chair.
"Excuse me?"
She sputters for a second.
"For months, I have been trying, Cass,
to be nice
and give you room to
be a teenager—
do your moody thing.
And you've been so angry—
so mean to me.
I know things are hard with everything
going on right now.
But you can't
treat me like this.
I don't deserve this.
We have to think about your dad.
You have to think about your dad
and not just about what you want.
I care more about him than baseball.
Don't you?"

THE TRUTH COMES OUT

Her words stop me.
Stretch me out,
thin as taffy.
For just a moment,
till I snap back in anger.
Because I care about Dad too.
But what about me?
What about my genes?
My future?

"Dad's the only one you care about."

"That's not true.
You know that's not true."

"How can I know if anything's true with you?
You've been keeping secrets all summer!"

Her eyes go wide.

I throw my crumpled napkin ball
onto the table
and run away.

SEPARATE ROOMS

Our apartment is small
and cramped.
It's the only thing we can afford
this close to the hospital.
The only way to get some space
is in my own room.
So I slam my door,
even though my heart hurts from yelling at Mom.
Like I picked up
the big, frozen secret
and hurled it across the frigid waters
between us.
But it shattered into my heart too.

Maybe Mom and I aren't
as far apart
as I thought.
I pull out a sheet of green kite paper,
fold a diamond.
Then a blue piece.
Another diamond.
Over and over in every color of the rainbow.
Tape them together to make a window star.
The light streams through it
from the setting sun,
and shines into
all the little cracks inside me.

Cracks I can't cover anymore.
Cracks I can't mend.
Cracks I don't want Dad to see
or Mom to fill with positivity.
No more paper smiles.
No more silly jokes.
I close my eyes,
spread my arms along the windowsill,
soak up the sun, and
try to tape myself back together.

CLEANING

Mom doesn't knock on my door.
She busts in,
surveys my room.
I can tell she's
marching around picking up every speck
of dirty laundry she finds.
I stay spread across the windowsill,
head against the glass.
Then she comes back.
This time
with the vacuum.
The monstrous noise fills the room until finally
she unplugs it. My carpet is probably spotless.
I say nothing in the sudden silence.
I don't even ask
if she needs help.
I keep looking out the window.
And then again
I hear her.
Wiping the doorknobs,
the light switch,
the walls.
Until finally she stops,
and I hear the creaking of bed springs.
"There's nothing left to clean," I mutter.
"You can go now."
She sighs.
"I'm not here to clean."

APOLOGIES

I turn around
and face her.
Really face her.
She smiles.
Paper smile.
Shaky smile.
Then stops,
shudders,
swallows.
Her eyes look above me,
beyond,
then straight down
deep inside me.
"I'm
sorry.
It's hard,
exhausting,
to care for your dad.
To raise you.
To do both at once."
She blows the bangs
out of her eyes
and gives me a smile—
not a paper one.
This one's different.
I think it's real.
"I've never told anyone that before," she says.
"But it's true.
It's hard to be a wife
and a mom.
And so many times I get it wrong.

Like now,
when I underestimate you."
She watches me, then says again,
"I'm sorry."

For one second
I think
of a joke.
Search
for a smile.
Until I remember
I'm done with that.
And all I have left
are cracks
and anger.
I turn and pound
my palm against the glass.
Again.
Again.
Hear the echo roar.
It sounds like hurt.
And it sounds like pain.
Something is about to shatter—
to crack.
It's not the window.
It's me.

"I'm sorry," I cry.
"I'm sorry.
I'm sorry.
I might be broken."

LET'S GO TALK TO DAD

"Let's go talk to Dad."
I think maybe Mom means,
Let's go yell at Dad.
Even though you're not supposed to yell
at someone with cancer.
But when we get to the hospital
and stand outside his room,
Mom says,
"Wait here for a bit, Cass.
Your father and I need to talk
in private first."
And this time, I know
that *private*
is code for
fight.
Mom closes the door behind her,
and I lean my ear up close to try and hear
but it's impossible.
I wait,
      and wait,
           and wait
for as long as I can take.
I can hear some noise
through the door
enough to know that voices are raised.
I gently,
silently
open the door
just a hair.

THEIR CONVERSATION

"I'm her mother! I can't believe you
both kept this from me."

> "Cass asked me to."

"That makes it worse! You're an
adult, Sean. You say no."

> "It didn't feel like the
> right thing to do."

"I feel . . . so . . . hurt. I'm not
—am I a bad mom?"

> "What? No! It's just . . ."

"What? Why would neither of you
talk to me about this?"

> "You're so positive sometimes."

"You think I *want* to be positive
all the time? I'm positive for you!"

> "Sometimes we just
> want to be sad."

Silence.

> "Come here.
> Come here.
> You are the best wife
> and the best mom."

"I try so *damn* hard."

"I know.
We know.
You're amazing.
I'm sorry, Jess.
I really am.
I should have told you.
After everything you've done for us
you deserved to know that she knows."

More silence.
I open the door wide enough
to stick my head through.
See Mom lying
curled up next to Dad
the way they do at home
when watching movies in their bedroom.
Finally Mom stops sniffing and clears her throat.

"Well, what do we do?"

"I think we let her decide."

"What? We can't just drop that in her lap."

I JOIN THE CONVERSATION

"I'm right here," I say.
"And I'm twelve.
It's already in my lap.
And I've made a pros-and-cons list."
I hold out the paper
so Mom can read.
Her hand goes to her lips.
She runs her fingers
through my hair.

I don't pull away.

"I can decide for myself.
But I wouldn't mind a little help."

INFORMATION

Mom's mouth pinches together.
Her eyes dart
back   and   forth
between Dad and me.
And for just a moment,
I see
worry,
sadness,
pain.
But then it's gone.
She pastes her smile back on.
"Let's focus on the positive."
Dad groans.
"No," Mom continues,
"just listen to me.
This test is a blessing.
It can give Cass
information.
Help her make
decisions."
"Decisions about what?" asks Dad.
Mom waves a hand in the air,
trying to pull out the answers.
But her smile slips.
"Like . . .
well, what about a career?
Or children?"

"What do you mean?" I ask.
"How would the test help me
with children?"
Mom hesitates.
"That's . . . well . . .
we don't need to talk about that today."

But it's *my* gene,
my future,
my two paths.
and I deserve to know.

"Tell me."

PASS

Mom stutters.
And talks about passing.
Passing on the gene.

Passing on—
that's Mom's nice way
to say *dying*—
before my kids are grown.

Watching my own kids
pass.
Die.

Her paper smile blows away,
and I pass her
a tissue.

IF YOU KNEW

Dad and I sit there
while Mom cries.
And our eyes
ask the same question.
Dad clears his throat.
"If you knew about my gene,
about what our future held,
would you still
have married me?"
Mom stops crying.
"What?"
Then it's my turn.
"If you knew about my maybe gene,
about what my future might hold,
would you still
have had me?"
And the question left
unasked
rings louder than
the rest.
If we knew at the beginning
about how it all would end,
would we still be
us,
we,
a family?

THAT MEANS YES

Mom doesn't answer.
Dad doesn't answer.
I don't answer.
Our questions fly away,
reaching outward in an ever-growing spiral.
But we—
Mom,
Dad,
me—
converge.
Arms wrapping.
Heads nuzzling.
Tears falling.
And just when I think we can't be any closer,
cancer is there
pulling us in,
holding us tighter.

SECRETS

"No more secrets," says Mom.
"From now on. Okay?"
Dad smirks. "Oooh, well
if that's the new family policy,
I guess I'd better let you know now
that I'm
a superhero."
Mom laughs,
then hiccups.
Dad gestures around the room.
"All of this is just part of my
mild-mannered persona."
Mom shakes her head. "You almost had me fooled."
"So that IV bag?" I ask.
"Totally radioactive," Dad replies.
"It's power-boosting juice."
"Nice, but . . ." I put on a big, sappy smile.
"You never had me fooled.
You were always my hero."
Dad shakes his head,
pulls me in for another hug.
"Come here, you big cheeseball."

PROS AND CONS OF GETTING TESTED

Pros
1. It might be good news.
2. I can be part of the elephant study.
3. I will know to do as much as I can and live as much as I can now, before I get sick.
4. I can use it to make decisions. Good ones.

Cons
1. It might be more bad news.
2. There's nothing positive about having the gene.
3. If I have the gene, I'll feel sick every time I think about my future.
4. I might use it to make decisions. Bad ones.

SOCIAL STUDIES LESSON

Joint lesson today
with Alex and Jayla
to talk about
Hammurabi and his code.
Then it's our turn to make rules
and write them down on our own version
of stone tablets.
"Well, in my kingdom," says Jayla,
"I'm making a rule about not playing the same song
more than three times in a row."
Alex hums. "Then I'm making a rule
about no snoring during the night."
"Hey," Jayla shrieks. "I can't help that!"
I laugh. "I'm making that rule too."
Jayla gapes at me.
"You're not supposed to take his side!"
"But you snore so loud!"
And then Jayla is throwing bits of the clay
that we're supposed to make into
stone tablets
at me and Alex
while we try to knock them away with
popsicle sticks.
"New rule," Jayla says,
now that we all have clay in our hair.
"Everyone has to be nice to me.
Always."
Alex and I look at each other and laugh.
His eyes sparkle.
I never noticed that before.

DOES HAZEL UNDERSTAND?

"What if Hazel thinks you're just making music
like we do with the parrots?" Jayla asks.
We're at the zoo.
She holds out an apple,
and Hazel takes it.
I stomp—
pause—
pause—
stomp again.
Hand Hazel a carrot.
"Thank you!" I shout.
"I don't think volume
will make her understand any better," Alex says.
He doesn't give any food to Hazel.
Doesn't like the way
the thick hairs
on her trunk
scratch his hand.
"I need her to understand,"
I tell them both.
"Why?" they ask in unison.
Like only twins,
or maybe siblings—
I don't know since I don't have any—
can.
"Because . . ."

EUREKA (PART 1)

I search for the words,
the right words,
to explain how I'm
connected
to Hazel
by a bunch of genes that she has
and maybe I don't.
"Hazel gives her blood
every week
so scientists can study the way her body
fights cancer."
And when I say that word,
I can feel cancer's presence,
somewhere around me,
like when you know someone's
watching.
So I say the next part
extra loud
to make sure
cancer
hears.
"Right now
all we have to fight cancer
is poison,
cutting,
and fire.
And none of them works that great.
But elephants?

Their body is so good—
so good—
at fighting cancer
that if we can figure out
how they do it
and then figure out
how to get our own bodies to do the same thing—"
"Eureka," says Alex,
hushed and thinking.
I nod.
"Eureka."

ANOTHER IDEA

Dan's Tires is the place
that sends us to the World Series
every year.
Every
year.

What about Dan's Tires?
texts Jayla
as I'm putting on pajamas.
Maybe they can get you
private
box
seats.
Maybe.
Even though we're not
important.
Even though we're not
fancy.
We're just sick,
poisoned,
and aching
to hear the
crack
of a home run.

TALK ABOUT THE WORLD SERIES

"Can we talk about the World Series?" I ask Mom
as she blows out my candle before bed.
Maybe it's too soon after our fight.
But I don't want to waste
this closeness.
I already know I can no longer
waste time.
Mom sits on my mattress.
It creaks to the side.
She nods.
"I'm ready to listen
if you are."
And so I tell her Jayla's new idea
and about Dan's Tires.
Mom listens,
then gives me her side of things.
I really listen this time too.

TOO MUCH

One time when I was five,
I went to the circus with my parents
and grandparents.
And they each bought me a treat.
Cotton candy,
candied almonds,
chocolate bars,
pulled taffy.
I ate every
single
bit of it.
Because everyone was happy
and thankful
after Dad was declared cancer free.
I was five.
I pointed at everything, and they bought it,
smiling.
But after the dancing bears,
trapeze artists,
and clowns in cars were finished,
I clutched my stomach.
Nobody smiled.
I'd had too much of all the good things—
all the celebration,
all the smiles and thankfulness
that led to sugar and circuses.
I wonder if that's what Mom is trying to
express
when she says she thinks
I would be asking Dan's Tires
for too much.

EMAIL FROM ELENA

SOS! HELP!
Not only am I dying
from zucchini poisoning,
but my mom is making all of us
start guided meditation.
So I'm also dying
of boredom.

Blaine: what's guided meditation?

Jazz: its when u try rly hard
2 not think.
isn't that super easy for u el?

Elena: haha very funny.
pounds fist

Me: Watch out Jazz.
I don't need both of you dead.

Blaine: elena if you die,
can i have your iPhone?

Elena: No.

I will be buried with it.

A DAY OUT

The next day when I wake up, Mom is already
dressed
and waiting for me with a message.
She's been thinking about what I said last night.
She thinks I need to get out,
have fun,
feel a bit more grown-up.
We'll just make sure to disinfect everything
when I get home.
All of that is to say
that Jayla
is on her way
with Sister Rowan.
And today we'll take the train.
We've never done that before.

SISTER ROWAN

Sister Rowan teaches Young Women's at church.
She smiles when she sees me,
asks how I've been,
puts her arm around my shoulders.
"Thanks for doing this," says Mom.
"My pleasure," Sister Rowan replies.
We climb into the back of her van,
Cheerios in all the seats.
"Sorry," she says.
"I didn't have time to clean."
Jayla and I laugh
and crunch when we sit down.
On the drive to the train station,
Sister Rowan lets us pick the music,
and tells us
she knows that
she's not super hip.
So she'll give us some space
and sit a few seats behind us.
Jayla's toes wiggle.
I can't help smiling.
It's nice to feel
a little older,
a little cooler,

maybe even normal.

I WEAR A MASK

The people in the train
breathe in,
breathe out,
breathe in again.
I won't let the germs go home with me.
And so I wear a mask.

The looks on the train
flicker,
stare,
over and over,
until every eye has landed on my face.
Look away,
look back,
look away again.
Wondering why I still wear one.
Won't let them know it bothers me. So,
I wear another kind of mask.

My best friend
glares,
huffs,
over and over,
until she finally turns to me and asks,
"Do you have another one of those
so people will stop staring?
I won't let them
keep looking at you like that."
And so,
she also wears a mask.

TETHERBALL

I spy the cancer center
up on the hill
and feel a tug—
a connection.
My family hasn't always lived in Utah.
We used to live in Idaho,
but after the first visit from
cancer,
we moved to Utah.
And the next few times it visited again,
we ended up moving
closer
and closer
to Hope Circle.
My life is like a game of tetherball.
Hope Circle is the pole,
my family is the ball,
and cancer
is the rope.

HAZEL

Sister Rowan says she'll wait by the fountain
and read
while we do our thing.
She doesn't want to interrupt.
So Jayla and I make our way to the elephants.
To Hazel.
Because I need to see her again.
But something is different when we get there.
Four zookeepers, in their green shirts and khakis,
crowd on both sides of the fence
around a great, gray heap.
I push my notebook into Jayla's hands
and run.
Jayla's dad turns around at the sound
of my sneakers on cement.
"What's going on?" I ask. "What's wrong?"

WHAT'S WRONG

"It's Hazel," he whispers. "She won't get up."

"What do you mean she won't get up?"

"She's old," he says. "Oldest elephant in
North America, actually.
She's sore, and tired, and heavy.
We try not to let the animals get this way.
We've let her go on . . .
too long maybe."
I peek between the wires and see her wrinkled body
move up and down with each breath.
"What happens if she can't get up?"
Jayla's dad wraps his hand around a rope,
steadying himself.
"We'll have to put her down."

The whole world feels set aflame.

Around me the other vets are poking, prodding
with tools and with their voices.
I get down on my hands and knees,
crawl between their legs
until I get to a spot where I can see
Hazel's forest-fire sunset eyes.
And then I whisper.

WHAT I WHISPER

"Hazel,
get up.
Hazel,
get up.
You can't die.
There's still carrots,
kiwis,
and apples to eat.
I know you're tired
and sore
and old.
But I need you, Hazel.
I need you to tell me the secret,
to teach me how to not get cancer,
to give me hope.
So get up, Hazel.
Because I am you,
and you are me.

And we aren't going to die."

RISE

I've never seen a miracle.
Although I've read about them plenty.
The way Jesus said, "Rise."
And then people did.
People who were
old,
tired,
and sore.
I wonder if they shook
the way Hazel did.
If they let out cries of pain or determination
like her trumpet.
I wonder if you could feel
the earth tremble with power
the way I could
when Hazel
stood
back
up.

THE HOPE OF ELEPHANTS

She looks at me
once she stands steady.
Her ears flutter out beside her head,
and the fire in her eyes
falls straight on me.
All around, the vets and zookeepers are cheering.
Hazel slowly lifts
one foot in the air
and then brings it down
with a powerful
earth-shattering
THUD.
Pause.
Everyone is still cheering.
Pause.
So only I notice the next
THUD,
which is how Hazel finally—
finally—
says thank you.
Jayla comes up,
grabs my arm.
"Did you see that?" I whisper.
"She knows."
Jayla smiles. "Knows what?"

"That we're connected—
me and her."

I straighten.
Stomp—
pause—
pause—
stomp again.

"Thank you."

And as long as Hazel is here,
there is hope.
The hope of elephants.

THE SIGN

When you believe in God,
you're supposed to see signs of him
everywhere.
You're supposed to feel him
guiding you.
So I suppose it's fitting that God guided me today
through a sign on the train.

Dan's Tires.
Going above and beyond
to get you on your way!

On my way.
On my way to the Series.

It's not asking too much of Dan's Tires.
It says they go above and beyond
right there on their sign.
I pull out my phone,
save the number,
and hope.

VISITING HOURS

I don't tell Mom about my plan.
After dinner we head to the hospital
to drive around
Hope Circle
a few more times.
Dad is waiting in his room.
His face is pale.
Sweat beads above his eyes.
They have that look again.
The chemo look.
The one that means
Dad's far away.
Not really here at all.
There's a game on TV.
Another team
we definitely won't get to see
if I can't get us
private
box
seats.
Dad leans his head against the pillow,
rests his eyes.
I wait for him to come back
to visiting hours.
To focus his eyes
and really see us.
When he finally does,
I whisper the solution to the problem
that only I seem to think we have.

NODDING

Dad's nod might have been
a yes.
Or it might have been Dad
falling asleep.
Or it might have been his way of
pretending
he heard me,
even though he can't really
concentrate
through the pain.
But when I whispered my plan to him,
he didn't say "No"
or "Too much."
So I'm going for it.
I'm going to try.
I'm going to ask.

THE WORST THING

On a video call that night,
Jayla tries to say the words
that will prepare me
for the asking,
to get rid of
the shaking,
the fear,
the worry about it being
"too much."
"What's the worst thing that could happen, Cass?"
I give the obvious answer.
"They could say no."
Jayla narrows those dark-brown eyes
waiting for me to finish her thought.
So I do.
"And things would be
exactly
the way they are now."
"Exactly," she says.
And when I think about it,
it's sort of like
driving around my own
Hope Circle.

WASH YOUR HANDS

"Wash your hands," says Mom
the moment I wake up.
"Wash your hands"
when it's time to eat.
"Wash your hands"
when we watch TV.
"Wash your hands"
when I touch a library book.
I wonder if
by the end of this,
I'll have any hands left
to wash.

GROUP THERAPY IV

Blaine returns.
He sits in a corner
by himself.
"Still nervous about my mom," he says.
"I don't want to see her like that.
Not ever again."
When Ms. Holmes asks everyone
what advice they would give
to a kid whose parent was newly diagnosed,
the other lifers say:

"Wear sunglasses
so church people don't recognize you in public
and give you that pity face."

"Try to catch your dad's sweat,
because it's basically radioactive
and maybe it'll give you powers."

"All I'm saying
is that if you tell people your mom has cancer,
you can pretty much get away with anything."

But Blaine says, "Buy lots of hand sanitizer."

DAN

The Dan
from Dan's Tires
must be really important.
Because I can't talk to him on the phone.
I have to make
an appointment.
Speak to him in person—
face to face—
with something called
the board.
Even though his secretary tells me,
"Yes, Dan knows who you are."
But if he's that important,
maybe he's important enough
to get
private
box
seats.
So I schedule a meeting
for Monday morning
at ten.
That gives me four days
to practice asking for
too much.

LIBRARY

Mom says you don't really need
school
if you have a good
library.
Because everything you could possibly
learn
is hidden in there between the covers of a
book.
But today all I need to learn is how to
stand,
speak,
ask.
So I pick up books by curbside checkout.
The Science of Influence,
Speak Up,
and *A Good Kind of Trouble,*
because reading about Shayla in that last one
always makes me feel like I can do anything.

HELP FROM HEATHER

I'm reading,
studying
by Dad's bed
while he sleeps
and Mom eats
lunch upstairs.
Nurse Heather
walks in and
sees the books.
"What are you
preparing
to do, Cass?"
Dad's sleeping.
I tell her
about the
World Series
and the private
box seats
for just us.
"Wow, Cass. Those
are big plans."
She says it,
and I think
maybe she,
like Mom, thinks
I'm asking
for too much.
But then she
smiles and says,
"Need some help?"

I nod. "Yes."
Nurse Heather
hands me a
pen. "Write down
your reasons.
And then tell
them to me."

REASONS

Dad needs private box seats
to keep out germs,
to stay alive,
to be my dad,
and to go back to the Series
next year.
And he needs to go this year
because,
because,
because
we always go.
Always.
And there are just some things
cancer shouldn't change.

I look at my reasons
and hope
they're not as flimsy as
this piece of paper.
Stand up.
Clear my throat.

Cancer sits on Dad's hospital bed,
leans forward,
smirks.
So I give my speech
loudly
until cancer is nothing more
than a shadow.

PROS AND CONS OF GETTING TESTED

Pros
1. It might be good news.
2. I can be part of the elephant study.
3. I will know to do as much as I can and live as much as I can now, before I get sick.
4. I can use it to make decisions. Good ones.
5. If I know, I can practice being brave.

Cons
1. It might be more bad news.
2. There's nothing positive about having the gene.
3. If I have the gene, I'll feel sick every time I think about my future.
4. I might use it to make decisions. Bad ones.

THE ARGUMENT

I look up and see
Dr. Barry
standing in the doorway.
I don't know how long he's been there,
but he shoves his glasses
back up on his nose
and says to Nurse Heather,
"May I speak with you in the hall?"

If Dad thought he was going to sleep well today,
he is in for a surprise.
Because Dr. Barry
and Nurse Heather
aren't married
or even dating.
They don't have kids
who force them to take their disagreements
outside
or to the laundry room
to discuss in whispers
and hissing words
the way Mom and Dad do
when they don't see eye to eye
and don't want me
to hear.

The hallway explodes
into shouts of
death—
protect—

hope—
liability—
Dan's Tires—
Cass—
private box seats.
Then Mom
walks up
and tells everyone to leave,
before she turns to me
and says,
"That's enough, Cass."

WE HAVE ENOUGH

"We have enough."
That's what Mom and Dad keep saying.
And I agree.
Enough cancer to last four families
a lifetime.
Enough hospital days
to fill two years on a calendar.
Enough worry,
enough tests,
enough handwashing,
and enough broken plans.
But enough visits
to the World Series?
Not at all.
Not a chance.
But Mom and Dad keep talking.

"Understand?" asks Mom,
pulling me from my thoughts.
Dad reaches for my hand.
"I don't need the World Series.
I only need you."

UNDERSTAND

Yes, I understand.
But the World Series isn't
for Dad. It's for me.

YOUNG WOMEN'S ACTIVITY

Wednesday night is when all the
teenagers
at church
get together.
I haven't had the chance to go for a long time
because of germs.
Because of cancer.
But I know Mom hopes
I'll forget the World Series
if she gives me a little freedom.
So tonight I go
with a bag full of origami paper.
Because it's talent night,
and I have only one talent.
Jayla meets me at the door.
She's been here every week,
so I guess she knows the ropes.
Takes my arm in hers,
whispers in my ear,
"I'll tell you everything you need to know.
A few new girls have moved in.
Brought some more color to the group,
which is nice.
I'll introduce you."

INTRODUCTIONS

"That's Katy Aaron.
She's seventeen and really cool."

"Hi! You must be Cass!"

I nod.

"It's good to see you."

Her hair is sleek black,
smooth and curled
around her chin.
"I like your hair," I whisper.
She laughs.

"Really? I hate it.
When it's short I want it long,
when it's long I want it short."

Jayla and I keep going.
"That's Madison.
No, don't look at her.
She's fourteen
and really shy."
I look away,
but not before I notice
Madison's round face
and blue eyes staring out
from behind red hair.
"Oh, there she is."
Jayla gasps.
"Who?"
"Ana.
The prettiest girl
in the entire world."
I wish I could say Jayla was
exaggerating.

But she's not.
Ana's hair
c
    a
       s
          c
            a
              d
                e
                  s

down her back
past her waist.
Dark brown underneath,
gold on top.
Deep tan skin
and a perfect smile
that she flashes at us.
"I'm really glad you're here,"
Jayla says,
squeezing my hand.
"I feel like I fit in
a little more when
I'm with you."

So do I.

THE NEWEST

They used to call us
the Beehives.
That was the name of the class
for twelve-year-olds like me.
I wonder if it's because
my stomach buzzes
whenever I see the older girls.
Cooler, prettier, with makeup on their faces.
I sit next to Jayla—
even she's wearing makeup—
and stare at my shoes
while Sister Rowan introduces me.
Then I watch as
the older girls share their talents.
It doesn't seem fair to let
them go first.
They've had three,
four,
five more years of practice
to make their talents really impressive.
I want to hide my bag of paper.
I want to rip it to shreds.
Until Jayla stands up and shows the mobile she
made
with paper cranes.
I should have known
Jayla would bring paper too.
Then she tells a story.

THE PAPER CRANE STORY

Jayla says that in Japan,
after the bombs
that shook the world,
killed tens of thousands,
and ended the war,
there was still poison
in the air,
in the ground,
in people's bodies.
It was an open invitation,
and cancer
took full advantage—
came to stay
with so many.
One day it visited a girl—
a girl who didn't want to die.
She believed if she could fold
one thousand paper cranes,
she would get a miracle.
But she didn't get to a thousand
before cancer
finished her off,
crumpled her cranes beneath its feet,
and left for another place.

But that was not the end of the story.
It was only the middle.

Because now there is a garden in Japan
to remember all those lives
taken,
lost.
People fold paper cranes,
leave them there,
remember,
pray,
and hope.
Cranes are hope
to some people.

Elephants are hope
to me.

Hope is a powerful thing.

A THOUSAND PAPER ELEPHANTS

Jayla finishes her story
by talking about how one day
she'll take her paper cranes to Japan.
I stand up,
give everyone a piece of paper.
Their eyes follow me around the room,
stay on me when I stand up front,
take a deep,
wobbly
breath
and say,
"Today I'm going to show you
how to fold an elephant.
Elephants have twenty sets
of the cancer-fighting p53 gene."
They don't stare at me
like I'm crazy.
They stare at me
like they know and understand
exactly what that means.
Then we all get to work.
As I fold,
bend,
crease,
I think of Hazel,
hope
      rising.

OLDER

When I get home,
I dump my paper on my bed
and head straight into the bathroom.
If I'm going to start attending Young Women's,
I want to make sure
I look like I belong.
Pull out Mom's makeup bag,
sort through it.
Find the blush,
mascara,
lip gloss.
Put some on,
but just lightly this time.
So I still look like me,
only a tiny bit older.
Then I pull up the ends of my hair
to see how it would look
at different lengths.
Mom walks in.
"What are you doing?"

"Can I get a haircut?"
"How short?"

"To here," I say,
pointing to my chin.
"If you cut it short,
you'll wish it was long."
I look back at my reflection.
"Yeah,
that's what I've heard."

SELFIES

Jayla and I get together again
to do our makeup and hair.
(She just changed her braids today,
and they're short—
curling under her chin.
I guess we both had the same thought.)

After we take at least
a hundred
pictures of ourselves
and put them on Instagram,
she shows me some of the new posts
from the older girls at church.
They're all dressed up in orange and black,
paw prints painted on their cheeks,
ribbons in their hair.
Under each picture is a caption:
#homecoming.
"What's homecoming?" I ask.
Jayla shrugs.
"It's like a dance or something."
She scrolls through the pictures some more
but the word stays in my mind.

HOMECOMING

It sounds warm
and inviting.
Homecoming.
A thought grabs hold of me
so strong
I have to say it out loud.
"Do you think we'll go to a dance someday?"
"Of course," says Jayla,
still scrolling,
not even looking up.
"There are church dances all the time."
I shake my head and
put my hand over hers
so she has to look at me.
"No, like
homecoming.
Do you think we'll go to
a homecoming
one day?"
Jayla thinks for a few seconds,
leans her head to the side
so all her braids
swish
across her face.
"I don't know.
I mean
Alex probably wouldn't like the loud music.
What about you?

Do you think you'd go?"
And in that moment,
we're not really asking each other about
homecoming
at all.
But about high school
and homeschool.
Both.
And as warm as the word
homecoming
sounds,
it can't block out the chill
running up my back
when I think about what might happen
to homeschool
if Dad weren't here anymore.
"No," I say
a little too loud.
"I don't want to go."
Jayla smiles.
"Good. Me neither."
It was fun to think about for a moment.
But there's much—
too much—
good right here.
Why would we leave home
for homecoming?

THE LIMERICK GAME

We visit Dad early the next day.
He smiles when we walk in.
"I feel like a game," he says.
But we didn't bring any games.
"Hand me that paper and pencil."

Dad writes down a line,
folds the paper,
hands it to Mom
who does the same and hands it to me.
A few more handoffs,
and we
have a limerick.

THE HOLLENS FAMILY LIMERICK

There once was a cranky old skunk,
that had a truly bad funk.
So she took a dance class,
went straight to mass,
and then got locked in a trunk.

"That one makes a lot more sense than the last one."
Dad laughs.

He's still smiling
and whispering, "A skunk at mass,"
when he falls asleep.

HAIRCUT

The woman at the haircut place likes to talk.
On and on she goes
about everything.
She asks me questions about my life,
but I don't say much.
Sometimes it's nice
to have people not look at you
like a sad little puppy dog.
Or click their teeth and
say, "Oh no, I'm so sorry."
She eventually stops trying
and just
snips,
snips,
snips
in silence.
Until finally she turns me around
to face the mirror
and says,
"What do you think?"
I touch my curls
now bobbing around my chin,
framing my head like a halo.
Pull one out as long as it will go,
let it bounce back.
"I love it."
Sometimes change is good.

ALL GROWN UP

"Well, don't you look all grown up,"
Mom says as she drives me home.
"Do you like it?"
I nod
and brush away some of the
leftover hair bits
that cling to my neck.
That's when I feel it.
A bump.
Right at the edge of my hairline.
The place the stylist shaved off
to thin out my hair a bit.
A lump.
A new mole
I never noticed before.

An open door.
The two sides of me
start thinking.

It's nothing.
Everyone has a mole or two.
Is it still a beauty mark
if it's on my neck?

Doctors,
scans,
biopsies,
chemo.
A mole is just
the beginning.

KEEPING SECRETS

I was mad at Mom
for keeping secrets from me.
Now I understand.
I can't tell her this. Not now.
She might never stop cleaning.

EMAIL FROM ELENA

Did you know you can juice a zucchini?
It's just as awful as it sounds.

Jazz writes: yum yum.

Blaine writes: if you can juice Spam,
nobody tell my dad.
he's back to cooking.

I email just him: Is your mom sick again?

He doesn't write back.

HOLDING HANDS

Dad came home tonight,
holding my hand and Mom's hand.
The same way he walked into the hospital
on Monday.
The same way he'll walk back in two days from now,
when they'll pump more poison inside him.
But for now, he's back to being mine.
Back to being ours.
When Mom lights my candle tonight,
a little flame sputters,
flicks,
jumps,
but never blows out.
I think I understand what she meant
before
about having enough.
But enough doesn't mean
you can't want more.
More than cancer
and hospitals
and a future full of poison.

I touch the mole on my neck
and think about
all the things
I still want.

AWAKE

Mom shakes
me awake.
Helps me pull on clothes and
shoes,
brushes my hair.
The sun is still sleeping.
Her eyes are worried.
"Going to the hospital," she says.
"You're going to Jayla's.
I'm sure it's nothing.
They'll fix him up, and we'll be back soon."

KIDNEYS

Nobody thinks about peeing.
Not really.
Not until they can't do it anymore.
Like Dad
when his kidneys decide
maybe cancer is better than poison
and stop working.

PROS AND CONS OF GETTING TESTED

Pros
1. It might be good news.
2. I can be part of the elephant study.
3. I will know to do as much as I can and live
   as much as I can now, before I get sick.
4. I can use it to make decisions. Good ones.
5. If I know, I can practice being brave.
6. I'll know to go to the doctor about anything even
   a little weird.

Cons
1. It might be more bad news.
2. There's nothing positive about having the gene.
3. If I have the gene, I'll feel sick every time
   I think about my future.
4. I might use it to make decisions. Bad ones.

IN THE CAR

I think about telling Mom
about my mole.
Maybe she'll take me to the doctor too.
Get everything checked out
so I don't have to sit here worrying.
But she brought the Clorox wipes.
She disinfects the steering wheel,
the seat-belt buckles,
the dashboard,
just for good measure.
All while Dad says,
"Honey, it's fine."

But Mom knows it's not fine.
That's why she's cleaning.

I keep quiet.

ALEX

Alex answers the door
with Mrs. Jasper right behind him.
She waves at my mom,
but he starts right in.
"Cass, did you know
this is one of the rare times
you can see
five planets in the sky
at once?"
I didn't.
He lets me come inside,
pulls me into the kitchen,
where the light over the oven is on.
"Cass," he continues,
looking straight into my eyes.
"Your irises reflect a wavelength
of about four hundred sixty
nanometers."
I touch my mole.
"Are you sure it's not four hundred seventy?"
He smiles,
looks deeper.
"Maybe, but I don't think so."
Mrs. Jasper pushes him
aside
to give me a hug
and take my things.
"Have a seat
while I get you some cocoa," she says.
I sit at the table.

Alex
sits by the window next to a telescope
and watches me
instead of the planets.

Lately I feel like
Alex sees me as a
science experiment.
And he's waiting for something to
explode.
Confusing.
Dangerous.

But then I remember
the way he practices his piano pieces
over and over.
And I think,
Maybe he's watching me that *closely.*
Something to get
just right.
Maybe Alex also has
two sides.
Like me.

A DISTRACTION

After Mrs. Jasper hands me the cocoa
and leaves the kitchen,
I touch my mole.
I need a distraction.
"Can you show me?"
I whisper.
"Can you show me the planets?"
Alex jumps up,
opens the door, and says,
"You can see them with the naked eye right now.
No telescope needed.
I just pull it out because
it seems right to have a telescope
when you're observing astronomical phenomena."
"That makes sense," I reply.
Alex smiles,
and his eyes are brighter
than any sky full of stars.

BLANKETS

It takes three blankets to watch five planets.
One to soak up the dew on the blades of grass,
another to keep the first
wet blanket
away from your back,
and a third to go on top.
To shield you from the cool, clear air,
so perfect for watching stars
rather than thinking about kidneys
or cancer.

SMALL

Alex points out the planets:
Jupiter, Saturn, Venus,
Mars, and Mercury.
I feel disappointed.
"They look like stars."
Alex laughs.
"Isn't it all beautiful?"
"I guess," I say. "But I thought
they'd be bigger."
Alex laughs again,
then stops,
like he realizes this is one of those times
when it's not the right time,
and he's out of step
again.
He pulls a prism from his pocket.
"If they were bigger," he mumbles,
"they wouldn't sparkle."

In my mind I hear Dad,
feel him shaking me awake
at that World Series game.
Wake up, Cass.
You don't want to miss this.

TRUTH AT DAWN

After a few minutes
of watching,
waiting,
observing,
Alex finally says,
"I like you.
Your hair is pretty,
and you're smart.
Not as smart as me,
but smart."
I freeze
as the sun peeks over the mountains.
"Thank you," I whisper.
He sighs.
"You're welcome."

CAUGHT

"What are you two doing?" Jayla asks,
as she walks out the back door
rubbing sleep from her eyes.
I feel like I've been caught.
Hand in the cookie jar,
looking up at Mars.
"Nothing," I say,
rolling away,
out of the blankets,
into the dew.
"You should have woken me."
I say, "I know."
She asks, "Are you okay?"
"I think so."
One last look at Alex. And the sky,
where planets are stars.
So much is simple
and complicated.
Two opposite things at the same time.

BREAKFAST

Jayla's mom hustles everywhere around the kitchen.
Her face wears a smile that won't shake off.
I know it's for me.
"Heard from your mom," she says.
"She thinks your dad is going to be
just fine.
Fluids is all.
Just needs fluids.
Gonna do some scans and send him home."
Alex scribbles on his whiteboard,
looks up.
"What's the prognosis for continued treatment?"
"Hush," says his mom.
"Hush, now."

I run my fingers
over the back of my neck.
Feel the bump
that could mean everything
or nothing.
Hush, I tell the fears
boiling up inside me.
Hush, now.

PRACTICE

"Have you thought about what to say
to Dan's Tires?" Jayla asks.
We're sitting in her room,
yellow curtains blowing,
posters of cities and
pictures of landscapes
covering every inch of space.
Like the whole world is crowding into
this single room.
"I don't think I'm going to Dan's Tires," I whisper.
"Mom says I have enough.
We have enough."
And those words battle.
Enough.
Too much.
Enough.

WHAT WOULD IT TAKE?

"What would it take?" Jayla asks.
"To convince your mom?"
I shrug and put my finger on
one of Jayla's postcards,
the ones she keeps of all the places she wants to go
one day
when she's on her own
and doesn't have to worry about whether things are
too loud
or too fast
or too much
for Alex.
She collects them like memories
she doesn't really have.
Holds on to them like a dream
she's not willing to give up.
I know why she's asking me—
why the World Series means something to her.
It would be another postcard,
another place to think about when her mom is at
therapy appointments,
trying a new diet for Alex,
or making sure everything is just right
for him.
I take my finger off the Disneyland postcard
and say, "A guarantee.
My mom wants a guarantee that
if we go to the Series,
everything
will be okay."

GUARANTEE

"But how can you give her that?"
Silence is my only answer.
Because there's no such thing
as guarantees in life.
A number you can call when things don't go right.
Get your money back
if you're not fully satisfied.
If there were,
my family would be rich,
living on a mountainside
in a mansion
or two.
But there are no returns.
No exchanges
because this life is broken
or the wrong size.
And so there's nothing
that will convince my mom.

In this world.

I look up at
Jayla's paper cranes
hanging from the ceiling.
They give me an idea.

WHAT ABOUT A MIRACLE?

"What about a miracle?"
That's what I ask Jayla.
She wrinkles her nose.
"You can't guarantee a miracle."
"Maybe not," I say.
"But I can try.
Maybe I can fold one thousand paper elephants.
Get a miracle.
Go to the World Series."
Jayla leans back on her bed,
watches her cranes twist
and turn.
"A miracle," she whispers.
"It's worth a try."

THE FIRST FOLD

When I make the first fold,
I can't help thinking
of the story Jayla told.
About the girl in Japan
and her one thousand paper cranes.
The mole on the back of my neck
seems to pulse
along with my heartbeat.
I wonder if that girl believed from the very
beginning.
Or if she always knew
what was in store for her.
Did paper feel to her
the way it feels to me?
Like magic
and possibility?
Or did it simply
erase
the pain of the moment?
Allow her to focus
on
one
thing.
This fold.
This bend.
This crease.
Instead of all the future
she might not see.

NO SUCH THING

Jayla and I have folded
ten elephants
altogether
when Alex walks in.
He sits beside me,
watches my fingers press the paper
and smooth the edges.
"What are you making
so many for?" he asks.
"Don't worry about it," says Jayla.
But I figure it can't hurt to have a little more help.
So I hand him a piece of blue paper
and say, "We're making enough elephants
for a miracle."
Alex is quiet.
He copies my movements
and ends up with
a lopsided elephant.
Holds it on his palm and says,
"This won't make a miracle, you know.
It's just paper."
I don't say anything.
Just keep folding.
Jayla rolls her eyes.
"I knew you wouldn't understand.
Go away."
Alex puts the elephant down,
picks up more paper,
does the first fold,
says,

"Do you know you can't see
most light?
There's all kinds.
Infrared.
Ultraviolet.
I bet there's some people
who don't believe in ultraviolet light.
But they still get sunburns."
Alex keeps folding,
copying my hands.
But Jayla stops,
puts down her paper,
and smiles at Alex.
A smile he doesn't see,
but I hope he can feel.

JAYLA TAKES ME HOME

Mom texts
to let me know they're home.
Jayla walks with me
the three blocks
back to my house.
She holds my hand
the way we used to when we were little.
"I'll keep folding," she says.
"Promise."
But out on the street,
with cars and buses zooming by,
miracles feel far away
and silly.
She drops me off at my apartment,
hugs me goodbye,
walks back to the home
she can't escape
and loves more than anything.
To pore over her postcards of all the places
she can't go,
and to love on the brother
who's keeping her from
exploring.

SOMETHING'S WRONG

The house smells like bleach when I walk in.
So I know
without having to see Mom's face
that something is wrong.

"What is it?" I ask.
"What happened?"

And when Mom looks at me,
I have to drop the bag of elephants
and sit down on the couch
because she's not wearing
her paper smile.

SCANS

They took scans of Dad's body
to check his kidneys
and found something worse than
plain old being tired of poison.
They found cancer
sneaking around,
hand in the cookie jar,
babies in cupboards and drawers.
Which means two things:
the chemo isn't working,
and this is our last
chance at a
World Series.

LASTS

Lasts are important.
Last piece of cake.
Last Uno card in your hand.
Last day of treatment.
Last chance to catch a fly ball,
or sing "Take Me Out to the Ball Game."
I'm not supposed to be having lasts.
This is still supposed to be the beginning.
And if we don't get
one last
World Series,
then it means
last year
was the last time.
And you should know something is
the last
when you're doing it,
so you can hold on to it more.
Like a postcard
for the rest of your life.

WHERE'S BLAINE?

I check my email but
there's still no message from Blaine.
I hope he's okay.

P53

p53: The Gene That Cracked the Cancer Code
is still sitting on my desk.
The cover starting to get
dusty.
I've tried to read it.
But it's not easy.
I couldn't even get past
the prologue.
But when everything around you
feels like it's
crumbling,
sometimes books can hold the world
together.
So I open to chapter one
and read the quote
under the heading.
Tumours destroy man in a unique and appalling way,
as flesh of his own flesh which has somehow been
rendered proliferative, rampant, predatory,
and ungovernable.—Peyton Rous

TRAITOR

Dad's body
keeps turning on him,
betraying him,
trying to kill him.
How can I love him so much,
but hate every cell in his body?

I wish I were a piece of paper
so I could rip myself
apart
into little tiny pieces,
sort through them,
find the bad ones,
then discover a way
to glue myself back together.

I
close
the
book.

RAGE

It starts as a buzzing somewhere in my chest.
Builds up like a swarm of bees,
growing,
growing,
growing.
Until it bursts into my stomach,
down my legs and out my arms.
A throwing,
kicking,
burning,
shaking.
Waves and waves crashing against my brain.
It burbles,
bubbles,
pushes,
and finally wrenches from my throat.
A growling, howling cry.
I scream into the air,
at the ceiling,
at the sky.
I pound into my pillow,
the carpet,
the earth.
Dig my fingers into my palms.
Deeper,
deeper still.
I want to smash the window.
I want to punch the door.

I want to break this whole wide world
in two.

WHAT'S WRONG?

"What's wrong?" Mom asks
as she walks into my room.
Paper is strewn all over the floor,
and I am in the middle,
sobbing.
"Everything is wrong!" I yell.
"Can't you see that?"
Mom walks to my bed,
straightens the pillow and fixes the sheets.
"Stop cleaning! Just stop!"
She stops.
"I don't know what else to do," she says.
"I don't know how else to help."
She sits down on the floor next to me,
And I curl in her lap like when I was a baby.
I wish I were a baby again.
I wish I weren't twelve.

"I have a mole," I whisper.

"What?"

"I
have
a mole."
I point to it.
My finger shakes.
"I have a mole," I say again.
"And we are unlucky.
We are unlucky.
We are unlucky."

NOTHING

Mom searches my neck,
finds the bump,
stares at it for a few seconds,
then runs her fingers through my hair.
I can feel her shaking,
hear her sniffling.
I don't look up.
Because as much as I
hate
her paper smile,
I'm even more scared
to see her cry.

"Am I dying?" I ask.

"No," she whispers.
"You're fine.
It's not
discolored.
It's just a regular mole."

"Then why are you crying?"

"Because I don't want to live this way."
And that feeling,
where my heart stretches thin
and my stomach twists,
floods me all the way through when I say,
"Me neither."

TEXT TO JAYLA

I'm going to the meeting
at Dan's Tires.
We're going to the Series.
As I wait for her reply,
I imagine myself there.
The crack of the bat,
the ball zooming through the air,
the familiar push of bodies all around me.
In my daydream,
I turn my head and there's Dad,
smiling.
Should we get nachos? he asks.
I love baseball nachos.
The kind you get in a hat.

My phone buzzes.
It's Jayla.
Good. I bought you a train ticket
and put it in your backpack
when you were here.
Just in case, you know?
Get off at
the 500 East exit.
Dan's Tires is right there.

I always knew
I could count on Jayla for
everything.

NOT TONIGHT

I sit on Dad's bed,
hold the blue book
with gold writing on the cover.
I promised to have faith for two
and it seems like
now
is the kind of time
when Dad needs faith the most.
"Can we read this tonight?" I ask.
Dad looks
then growls,
"No."
I run my hand over the cover.
"You don't have to read.
I can read it to you."
I open to the place I marked
earlier.
The psalm that used to be his favorite.
"The Lord is my shepherd;
I shall not want."
"I said no, Cass."
He doesn't yell it.
He never yells.
But still his words
cut,
slice,
sever.

PROS AND CONS OF GETTING TESTED

Pros
1. It might be good news.
2. I can be part of the elephant study.
3. I will know to do as much as I can and live
   as much as I can now, before I get sick.
4. I can use it to make decisions. Good ones.
5. ~~If I know, I can practice being brave.~~
6. ~~I'll know to go to the doctor about anything even~~
   ~~a little bit weird.~~

Cons
1. It might be more bad news.
2. There's nothing positive about having the gene.
3. If I have the gene, I'll feel sick every time
   I think about my future.
4. I might use it to make decisions. Bad ones.
5. I will always be scared.
6. Going to the doctor doesn't matter.
   Dad's still dying.

REDO

It's late—
past midnight probably—
when Dad walks into my room.
He wakes me up when he sits on my bed.
"I'm sorry," he whispers.
"Can we have a redo?"

GENTLY

Dad's hand is bony,
white,
and shiny.
I cradle it in mine
as his voice, so soft—
velvet
smooth—
whispers our poem for the night.

"'Do not go gentle into that good night,
Old age should burn and rave at close of day;
Rage, rage against the dying of the light.'"

Out my window in the dark night,
the stars (and planets) burn and shine as if to say,
Stay, stay Dad; don't ever leave my sight.

"You can't go gently." I say it out loud.
"You have to fight and burn against your death.
Live, live, and never quit or go without a sound."

Dad closes the book.
"I won't," he says.
"I swear I won't."
And even though he whispers it,
his words are full
of thunder.

EMAIL FROM JAZZ

She sends a meme
of a man reading a tiny piece of paper.
The text says:
THINGS THAT DON'T CAUSE CANCER.

Elena writes back:
Zucchini.
That list says
zucchini.

SUNDAY

On Sunday,
boys from church come
with masks on
and gloved hands.
They break the bread,
kneel,
pray.
We eat it, and I think about
Jesus bleeding,
dying,
healing all those sick people,
but not healing my dad.
The book of scripture
still sits by the rocking chair
unopened,
stuck shut between all Dad's
worries,
doubts,
anger.
But if Dad is dying,
I think he needs scripture now
more than ever.

BASEBALL ON SUNDAY

We usually don't play
baseball on Sundays.
But it seems like today
it might be okay to break that rule.
Dad carries the bat.
I carry the gloves.
But halfway across the street,
I take the bat too.
It's too heavy for Dad.
"I just need to catch my breath," he says
when we walk onto the diamond.
So we both sit down
next to home plate.
"Do you remember that time," Dad says,
"when you caught your first pop fly?"
I nod.
"I was so proud of you."
I lean my head against his shoulder,
stare off into the outfield.

We remember together.

HAVE TO ASK

"How's your list coming, Cass?"
Dad asks
later, when we're lying in the grass.
I sigh
and watch the clouds go by.
My throat gets dry.
"No answers yet."
"I bet."

I know I shouldn't ask, but . . .
"Dad, do you still believe
in 'If you ask, you shall receive'?"
I wait and listen to him breathe.
"Cass, we should go."

But I'm not ready.
"No.
Tell me something I don't know."

WHAT DAD DOESN'T KNOW

"How about today," says Dad,
"I tell you the things *I*
don't know?"

"Okay."
I wait
while Dad gathers his thoughts.

"I don't know how televisions work.
I've tried, but
they're confusing."
"Me too." I laugh.
"And I don't know
what my favorite book is.
There are too many—
far too many—
to love."
I nod
because it's true.
"I don't know if you should get the test.
I got it, and now
I'm scared
all the time.
Is that a life?
That's another thing I don't know."

I hold my breath
because I don't know either,
and the questions suck the air
right out of my chest.

"And sometimes, Cass,
I don't know if I believe in God.
Why would Heavenly Father,
Heavenly Mother,
saddle people—
their children—
with so much pain?
Sometimes I feel
betrayed.
Like I've tried
                    and tried
                                and tried
to do everything right.
And look where it got me.
Got us."
I am quiet
like in testimony meeting.
Because what Dad just said feels
the same to me as when Mom
stands at the pulpit
and cries
about how much she loves Jesus.
I grab Dad's hand.
"It's okay," I whisper.
"I'll have faith
enough
for both of us."

TEXTING BACK

Baseball with Dad
makes me think about
my team
and all the missed calls.
I saved the voicemails
even though I was too scared
to call back.
I don't know if I'm braver now
or just lonely enough
to really need my team.
But I start with Coach.
Just a text.
>   Hey Coach. This is Cass
>   from baseball. I just wanted
>   to say thanks. For everything.

A minute later, my phone buzzes.
*Cass, I've been thinking
about you. How's your dad?*

I sigh. How much should I say?
>   I don't know. We'll find out more soon.
It's the truth.
Well, keep me in the loop, okay?
>   Okay.
It's a short conversation,
but still
it reminds me
I'm not alone.
I have a team.

WHICH MIRACLE?

That night,
I fold three elephants
before I sleep.
Mom comes in,
switches off my lamp,
lights the candle.
"More elephants?" she asks.
"One thousand elephants," I whisper back.
"I'm trying to fold
a miracle."
Mom balances an elephant
in the palm of her hand
and says,
"Which miracle?
You or Dad?"
My heart pulls like taffy
because I was only thinking
about the Series.

BACK

On Monday it's back to Hope Circle.
Round and round we go.
But Dad isn't here for treatment.
He isn't here for poison.
He's here to make sure that what they saw on the
scan
is really cancer.
He's here waiting
for someone to say,
"Yes, sir. You're really,
truly
dying."
Until someone says that—
says it for absolute sure—
we hold on to a little string of hope,
like a necklace that
we rub until it shines.
Dad's genes make his body grow
all sorts of tumors.
Not just cancer ones.
And we're praying—
Mom and me—
to hear the most beautiful word
in the whole, wide world.

Benign.

BEFORE WE LEFT

I sent an email to the lifers.
I'm doing something hard today.
Cheer me on?

NURSES' STATION

Nurse Heather
lets me join
her at the
nurses' station.
She says she'll
teach me how
to listen
to heartbeats—
take someone's
blood pressure—
and we'll call
it homeschool.
Mom thinks that
sounds like a
great idea.
Anything
to distract
me from
remembering
about Dad
and dying
and lasts.
But I'm not
distracted.
Just waiting
for the right
time to leave.
Because there's
a ticket
in my pocket.

And a train
just outside
the hospital.
And when the
time is right,
I'll be on it.

A LITTLE

At the nurses' station
I tell Heather about
my meeting.
About how this will probably be
the last Series
for us.
And how I wish
that last year
when we sat outside,
I'd opened my eyes
a little wider.
Sung
a little louder.
And reached up
a little higher
for that home-run ball.

DR. BARRY

Dr. Barry walks by and stops
when he hears me talking about the World Series.
"You're not still thinking
that's a possibility,
are you?"
He pushes his glasses back on his nose.
Asks some nurse named Marsha
for bloodwork,
then turns back to me
and waits for an answer.
"I don't know," I say.
He stares harder at me,
makes me feel like a worm
drying on the sidewalk
when the sun comes out after the rain.
I clench the train ticket
in my pocket.
"I guess not."
Dr. Barry nods. "Good."
He looks at Nurse Heather.
"I'm glad you finally came to your senses about this."

QUIET

As Dr. Barry walks away, the only sound
on the whole floor
is the *clip-clop*
of his shoes on the tile.
All the nurses hold their breath,
waiting,
watching.
Nurse Heather scribbles in someone's chart
extra hard.
"Georgia," she says
to a tall nurse in purple scrubs.
"Do you think anyone here
could take over my patients for
the last hour of my shift?"
Georgia nods and says,
"You go show
Dr. Barry
who needs to come to their senses."
Nurse Heather takes my hand
and walks me toward the exit.
"Don't look back," she says.
"Don't say anything.
I'm going with you."

DRIVING

Nurse Heather drives out of the parking garage
like she's escaping prison.
Hands on the wheel
turning white.
Finally
she breathes
and pulls a piece of paper from her pocket.
"You better get practicing."

EMAILS FROM THE LIFERS

Elena: Whatever it is,
you can do it!
Jazz: rah rah rah
goooooo cass!

Still nothing from Blaine.

THE DOOR

We get there
just in time.
I might've been late if
I'd taken the train.
"They're waiting for you,"
says the man at the desk.
"Go on in."
Nurse Heather leans down
and whispers in my ear,
"You deserve this chance."
As I turn the doorknob,
I realize
that nobody ever knows if they're asking
too much
without the actual
asking.

In my head, I remember Dad
pulling my hands away from my face
when I was scared of fly balls
at the Series.

*If you're scared the whole time, Cass,
you'll miss the best parts.*

DAN AND THE BOARD

There is no board
in the room,
only a long table
with people sitting around it.
And a man standing
at the far end.
I know who he is
even before he says,
"Welcome. I'm Dan Bryson."

PRACTICE

The only time I've practiced
what I'm going to say
before today,
Dr. Barry said
no.
Now I can't remember anything,
and my paper looks all smudged,
blurry,
and wrong.
A woman at the table
clicks her pen
up and down,
and says, "Go on.
Tell us what you came here for."
And those two words—
tell us—
change everything.
I'm not asking.
I'm telling
a story.
My story.
One with two different paths
and only one
traveler.

MY STORY

"Eight years ago,
you started sending my family
to the World Series every year.
Because my dad gets
cancer
the way some people
catch a cold.
He has it again.
But this time
he's getting chemo
at the same time as the Series.
And Dr. Barry says
he can't go.
He'll die from all the germs.
Maybe next year.
That's what everyone says.
But now Dad's . . .
he might be . . .
we don't know for sure,
for sure.
But it looks like . . .
there won't be a next year.
There won't be a next anywhere.
It's this year
or never again.
But I have a plan.
Private
box
seats.

With only me,
Mom,
and Dad.
Nobody else.
To keep the germs away.
I know it's expensive,
and I know it's
'too much,'
after everything you've done for us.
But my dad's life—
that might be my future too.
Because of a gene.
And if my world isn't going to fill up
with firsts,
I'd at least like it to fill up
with lasts
I can hold on to."

IN THIS MOMENT

The clock ticks—
one,
two,
three,
four
seconds on the wall.
Four whole seconds
of waiting
for a yes
or no.
And in those moments,
once again
I'm a cat in a box.
Both going and not going
to the Series.
Schrödinger's Cass.

HOW DO YOU FEEL ABOUT THAT?

The same woman speaks first
with a click of her pen.
"It's a lot of money,"
she says.
Click
click,
goes the pen.
"Is it even possible?"
says someone else.
Dan nods.
"We'd have to buy out a corporate box.
But enough money
always talks."
Click
click,
goes the pen.
"High cost," says the woman.
"Not a lot of reward.
No offense," she says to me.
"This man was a good employee," says Dan.
"I treat my employees well.
Not everything can be measured
in dollars and cents."
Click
click,
goes the pen.
"But you can't even advertise it," says the woman.
Dan stands up.
"Now hold on.
That's a good idea."

He leans on the table
and everyone else
leans toward him.
Even me.
The pen falls
silent.

"What about a fundraiser?
Everyone comes to buy tires,
but the money goes to you.
And we can ask for donations from local businesses.
Hang their signs around the building.
How do you feel about that?"
All eyes turn to me.
How do I feel?
It feels like all my ideas
rolled into one
great
big
possible
miracle.

MAYBE

When I leave the room
with Dan and the board,
that's not a board at all
but just a bunch of people,
I have an answer
to my asking for too much.

Maybe.

It means there are a lot of ifs.
If we can buy out a corporate box.
If we can raise the money.
If people show up to the fundraiser.
And the biggest if of all,
the one I don't tell them about.
If Mom says yes.

MOM'S ANSWER

"A fundraiser?
We don't even know
if we can go."
Nurse Heather explains
about special masks,
the gloves,
the disinfectant we'll carry,
the signs telling people
not to come in.
How we'll get there early
and leave late.
Never touch a person.
Never see a germ.
Mom's lips pull apart
with her answer sitting on her tongue,
when Dad says,
"Absolutely, we'll go."
And that becomes
Mom's answer too.

TEXT TO JAYLA

Think you can help me
raise funds for the World Series?

Is Morocco a country?

That means yes.

EMAIL FROM BLAINE

sorry i haven't written.
i had a cough and a fever
and had to stay in my room
away from everyone.
i hope your hard thing went okay.

What do I say
to that?
I'm sorry.
How are you feeling?

I don't know how he'll answer,
if he'll take off his armor.
But I decide right then
that if he does,
I will too.

WAITING FOR RESULTS

It can take a week
to get the results of a biopsy.
A week to find out
if Dad's living
or dying.
A week of being a cat in a box.
It's just long enough
without the chemo in his blood
for his stomach to feel settled,
his energy to start returning.
For everything to seem normal.

Most people think the waiting is hard.
But I wouldn't mind staying here
a little longer.

Where nothing's for sure, and we can all pretend
that nothing has to end.

But there's a due date on this time.
We can't keep it forever.
And we'll never be ready.

CALLING JACK BACK

Jack doesn't have his own phone
so I can't text him.
Have to actually call,
talk to his mom,
ask for Jack.
"Hold on," she says,
and a few seconds later
I hear his scratchy voice
come through.
"Hello?"
"Hi, Jack."
"Cass? Is that you?"
"Yep."
"Geez," he says,
but I can hear the smile in his voice.
"Dinosaurs have been extinct
almost
as long as it took you to call me back."
I laugh.
Apologize.
Then tell him about the fundraiser.
"Cool," he says. "I'll tell the team.
We're going to buy so many tires, Cass.
We'll have to—
I don't know—
build a whole park out of them."
It's not one of his funnier jokes,
but it still sounds pretty good
to me.

BIG PLANS

Dan's secretary calls me at least once a day
to let me know what's going on.
"We have it all set up," he says.
"We'll set aside a Saturday,
and everyone who comes in
will pay the usual price.
But we'll only take the
wholesale cost of the tires.
All that profit
goes straight to you.
Sound good?"

It sounds better than good.

"There's just one thing
we want you to help us with."

KNOW

The thing about fundraisers
is that they only work
if people know.
Know everything.
Know when it is,
where it is,
and most importantly,
why it is.
It means you have to put all the details of your life
on a flyer,
and hope,
hope,
hope
that it's enough to tug at someone's heart
and make them think,
"I should give that person money."

Dad hasn't written for his blog
since he got the scans.
But now the whole city will know
anyway.
And they get to decide
if my miracle
is worth it.

MATH LESSON

Mom likes to work math
into what happens every day,
rather than use a curriculum.
She calls it *life math,*
which Dad says is a cruel joke,
since he's always felt like doing math
might kill him.
Today I'm at the table
working out how many tires
we have to sell.
How many flyers
I have to post
to sell that many tires.
If ten people see each flyer,
and only fifteen percent of people
who see the flyer
go.
And how many miles
I'll ride on my bike
to post them
if I do an entire
ten-block radius.
When I'm finished,
I don't feel smarter.
But I do feel
a little more hopeless.

It's a lot of tires.
A lot of flyers.
A lot of ifs.

EMAIL FROM BLAINE

i'm lonely.
but mostly scared.
Cass, what if i get my mom sick
and she dies?

I take a deep breath
when I read those words.
Why does it feel
so brave for him to say it?
I want to be brave back.

I write: I worry about that too.
My dad might already be dying.
But for some reason
I can't do it.
Can't be brave back.
So I delete it all.
I try the kind of bravery
that's fake.
Paper-smile bravery.
It will be okay.
I bet your mom will get better.

I close my eyes when I hit send.
Whisper, "Sorry, Blaine."

ANOTHER WEDNESDAY

Days don't feel the same
when you're waiting.
They stretch and pull like rubber bands
then feel too hot
and snap.
You put on a paper smile
because for a while
you can pretend.
But something always brings you back
to worry,
to cancer,
to dying.
I should have known that Wednesday—
the best day of the week, zoo day—
would do the same thing.

IN THE CAR

I slide into the seat next to Jayla,
notebook in my lap.
Mrs. Jasper pulls out of the parking lot
and onto the crowded street.
"What are you girls going to see today?"
"The elephants," I reply.
"I want to see Hazel."

Nothing.

Jayla taps her pen against her notebook.
Her eyes say there's something I should know.
Her mom whispers, "Oh, my land."
But Alex gives it to me straight.
He doesn't beat around the bush.
He doesn't say it gently,
or lead with a joke.

"Hazel's dead."

NOT POSSIBLE

"That's not possible,"
I whisper.
"No. That's not supposed to happen."
Alex nods.
"It's one hundred percent possible.
Every living organism has to die.
Hazel was a living organism, and she completed her
life cycle."

"Shut up!" I yell.

Mrs. Jasper puts on the brakes.
Jayla's eyes get wide.
Alex pushes back into his seat and mumbles,
"If nothing died,
there'd be no room for new life."

"Shut up!
Shut up!
Shut up!"

MRS. JASPER PULLS OFF THE ROAD

"Maybe I should take you home."
I shake my head.
My eyes burn,
and my fingers clench.
Unclench.
I don't want to go home.
I want to see Hazel.
"No. Please," I whisper.
Mrs. Jasper sighs,
turns the wheel,
drives back onto the road.
I lean way, way over
so my head's between my knees,

and I begin to cry.

SILENCE

The car ride,
walking in the zoo,
making my way up the trail,
leaning against the wire fence,
then falling to the ground and staying there
until my tears mix with the dust,
creating tiny dots of mud
that only I see
in all this
silence.

A GOOD LIFE

Jayla is waiting on the bench
when I finally stand up.
"Are you okay?" she asks.
"I guess," I lie.
"She was really old," Jayla says.
"She lived a good life."

A good life.

She lived her life in a zoo enclosure.
She never went anywhere or saw anything.
Did she even have kids?
Did she love another elephant?
How can anyone say
anybody
lived a good life
when it's over?
How can anything truly good end?

She always had plenty to eat
and people to take care of her.
Kids who loved her
and fed her
kiwis,
apples,
mangoes.
And she shared part of herself
to help people like Dad.
She didn't die until she was old.
That actually seems pretty good
to me.

I nod.
But I don't say the hidden thing
deep down in my heart.
Hazel was supposed to help me
find the secret.
She was supposed to save Dad
and maybe me.
Now she's gone.

HARD

We sit there for a few minutes,
the chilly fall wind
blowing past our cheeks.
Jayla clears her throat.
"He was just trying to help.
Alex."
I try to listen.
Try to agree
that I was too
hard
on him.
But there is something
hard
in my chest.
"It was the wrong thing to say," I whisper.
"I know," says Jayla.
"But try not to be
too mad at him."
I try to forgive Alex.
I really do.
But it's just too
hard.

TRASHED

When I get home,
I go straight to my room.
Paper elephants line the windowsill,
the dresser,
the closet shelf.
I throw each one into the trash.
Trunk,
tusks,
and all.
Hazel couldn't save herself.
She can't save me.
Cancer
waltzes into my room,
sees my pile of paper elephants,
takes its foot,
and squashes them to pieces.

DO YOU BELIEVE IN MIRACLES?

"Do you believe in miracles?"
I ask Dad.
His eyes are brighter tonight.
Last bits of chemo drained away.
"Hmmm," he says.
Like that's an answer.
"Hmmmm."
He pulls out
Emily Dickinson
and reads.

"'FAITH is a fine invention
For gentlemen who see;
But microscopes are prudent
In an emergency!'"

"That sounds like something Alex would say."

"He's not always wrong."

"But he's not always right
either," I reply.
Dad smiles.
"Maybe not.
Let's see what else Miss Dickinson has to say about
the matter."
He reads.

"'Hope is the thing with feathers
That perches in the soul,
And sings the tune without the words,
And never stops at all.'"

Dad stops, bends,
and whispers in my ear.
"I don't know if there are miracles,
but there is always hope."

And then both sides of me
write a poem of their own.

Hope is the voice inside me
that whispers, "Life is good"
and tells me, "Aim high, reach out, try,
just like you know you should."

Hope is a word for those
who live life free of fear.
But tests and poison work
when cancer visits here.

SOMETHING TO HOLD ON TO

And here I am
all over again.
Two poems.
Two answers.
Two roads.
One traveler.
As I sink into bed,
I find myself hobbling between

faith   and   doubt

science   and   saviors

hope   and   microscopes.

And I search for
something,
something,
something
to hold on to.

But   there
is   nothing
here   in
the   middle.

Only Schrödinger's Cass.
Only me.

POSTING FLYERS

The flyers arrive on our doorstep.
A big orange stack
held together by plastic bands.
I put them in my backpack
and bike over to Jayla's
to ask for help.
She opens the door before I even knock.
I hear Alex in the house.
"He's flipping out," she says.
"Let's go."
And we do,
all the way to University Avenue,
where we hang a flyer
on every telephone pole,
bench,
and bus stop.
The pile of them
feels heavy in my backpack,
but also light
all at once.
Like

fear   and hope.

Sometimes I wonder
if I'll ever feel anything else,
or if all of life is just
hope
and fear.

TALKING ABOUT ALEX

Jayla's quiet right now,
except for the sound of the stapler.
Pound,
pound,
pound.
She smacks one extra hard
and sighs.
"Bad day?"
I finally ask.
"Bad day for Alex.
Bad day for everyone."
I bend the corner of a flyer
while Jayla goes
pound,
pound,
pound.
Alex's name makes my heart feel hard again.
As hard as Jayla's stapler.
"He told me he likes you," Jayla says,
and she stops.
No *pound.*
"I know," I say. "He told me."

"You like him back?"

LIKE EVERYONE ELSE

My heart turns harder until it finally
cracks.
"No.
No way.
Ew."
"Ew?" says Jayla.
"What's that supposed to mean?"
I push my bike
and mumble, "Every living organism has to die.
Why can't he just be normal and say he's sorry?"
Jayla doesn't push her bike
but stands there.
"He might not always say the right thing,
but at least he tries.
He tries to help.
You out of everybody
should know that."
She holds up a flyer.
"This is all because of him."
I look at her.
"I know.
But you even said
he's weird.
And somebody should tell him
it's not okay."
Jayla puts up a hand.
"He's like everybody else.
A little bit normal,
a little bit different.
What's so weird about that?"

NO ANSWER

Cars zoom by.
They drive past
with all the
"I'm sorrys"
I should be saying.
Jayla hands back
the stapler,
the flyers, and
wheels her bike away.
She stops,
turns,
and says,
"Don't you ever call him
weird
again."

"You always call him
weird," I shout.
Jayla yells back, "I'm
his sister. You're not."

RUN OUT

I run out of staples
before I run out of flyers.
I run out of energy
before I run out of anger.
I'm running out of people who understand,
but I'm not running out of problems.

Can I run out of this life
and into a new one?

BACK AT HOME

When I get back home,
I see it in their faces.
The results are back.

A LIST OF THE UGLIEST WORDS

Pus.
Pregnant.
Pulchritude.
Chunk.
Moist.
Ointment.
Bunion.

Malignant.

EMAIL FROM ELENA

Guys, I just had my first ice-cream cone in
FOUR MONTHS.
It was probably
the most delicious thing I've ever eaten.

Jazz replies: ooh, so i guess u wont be needing
this zucchini ice cream i just made

Blaine writes: i heard that meditating about ice
cream is just as good as eating it.

Elena: Jazz, there is something seriously wrong
with you. And Blaine, whoever told you that is
going to hell for lying.

Me: lol
It's the only thing
I'm brave enough to say.

LIVE YOUR LIFE

Dr. Barry sits in front of us.
He pushes his glasses up on his nose,
brushes his hands over the papers in front of him,
and says,
"You still have options.
We can try a different chemo.
But you were already on
the strongest one,
so that doesn't bode well.
There are always
trials
to sign up for.
Or last of all,
you can end treatment,
go home,
and live your life."

Live your life
is a funny way to say
go home and die.
As if living
isn't what we've been trying to do all along.
Isn't that what all the
poison
and hospitals
and trips around Hope Circle
are for?
So Dad could live his life?

TERMINAL

"I hate to use the word terminal."
That's what Dr. Barry said.
Terminal
is a funny word.
A word with two meanings.
Sometimes it means something is going to kill you
eventually.
It's terminal.
Words nobody wants to hear.
But a terminal is also
a room
in an airport
with big glass windows,
and hard, squished-together seats.
It's the place where you wait
to go somewhere new.
The place where you worry about
whether your flight will be on time,
who will meet you when you land,
if the pilot knows what he's doing.
It's the last place you see before you
step onto that plane
and shoot into the sky.
Ready for your next adventure.
I'd rather think of
terminal
like that.

TEXT TO JAYLA

It's malignant.
She texts back. *I'm sorry.*
I type, I'm sorry
then delete it
when I hear Alex's voice in my head:
every living organism has to die.
Jayla and I haven't tried
to meet in our dreams
for a couple days now.
If we did,
I'm not sure what I'd even say
to her.

FAMILY MEETING

Sitting around the table and waiting
for words to come.
Mom says, "Maybe we should say
a prayer."
Dad shakes his head.
"I think it would really help today," pleads Mom.
"Hasn't helped me yet," Dad replies.
"That's not true."
Dad stands up,
walks away.
And so we pray
without him.

MOM'S PRAYER

"Heavenly Father
we're thankful . . .
we're thankful . . ."
She stops
like she can't think of anything
positive right now.
Shakes her head,
keeps going.
"I need my husband, Lord.
Cass needs a dad.
You've saved him before.
Please save him again.
We need a miracle.
We're begging for a miracle.
Please.
Please."
Pause.
"Amen."

A GOOD LIFE

Mom leaves my candle burning longer tonight
than usual.
She sits on my bed,
and we stare at the flame.
"It's beautiful, isn't it?" she whispers.
"Candlelight.
I feel myself drawn to it,
and I can't look away."
I lean my head on her shoulder.
"Alex said that every life
begins
with a spark of light."
"I like that," says Mom.
"They say it ends that way too.
With a bright light."
"I don't want to talk about that," I whisper.
Mom sighs.
"I understand.
But whatever happens, Cass,
I want you to know
and remember
that your dad lived
a good life."

There are those words again.

"A good life?"
I practically spit.
"How could it be a good life?

It was filled with hospitals
and poison.
Cancer
and pain.
And it's ending.
It's ending!
How is that a good life?"

Dad stands in my doorway.
"Is that a bad life?"

DAD'S LIFE ACCORDING TO DAD

"My life has been filled with
long summers
and cool breezes.
You
and your mom.
Helping hands
and hopeful hearts.
Poetry,
literature,
and art.
Board games
and long walks.
Deep sighs
and deep talks.
And eight
trips to the World Series."

"But you're dying," I say.

Dad smiles.
"Everybody's dying, Cass.
Every single day."

FAMILY TIME

In the days after getting the call
and meeting with the oncologist,
I don't have time to worry
about the fundraiser
or about Jayla.
I think only about
Family Time.
But it isn't fun like it used to be.
Now it feels heavy.
Like a race in slow motion.
One of those races where
you fill up a sponge with water,
walk it some distance,
and squeeze to fill up a bucket.
And we're trying not to let
a single drop
slip out of the sponge
and land on the grass.
Because our bucket is running out of water.
So we soak up every second,
carry it around in our minds,
wring it out over
and over.
And hope that once the bucket's empty,
we'll have gathered
enough.

DAD'S DECISION

After three days,
Dad calls Mom and me to the front door.
"Let's go to the baseball field," he says.
But all he has is a blanket.
We put on our hats and go.
Turns out
it only takes one blanket
to lie in the outfield
and plan the rest of your life.
"I'm going to try the new chemo,"
Dad says
as we watch the clouds float by.
"But I also want
to live."

THE LIVING LIST

He pulls a small notebook
from his pocket
and writes.
See the Grand Canyon at sunrise.
See the Christmas lights at Temple Square.
Camp in Yosemite.
Feel the ocean on my feet.
Then he hands the list to Mom
and she writes.
Go back to the place we met and buy an ice cream.
Read Les Mis *together and actually finish it this time.*
Sink our hands into cement when nobody's watching.
Dad laughs and gives the list
to me.
I try to think of things I want to do with Dad
before he dies.
Learn to drive.
Go to college.
Have someone ask him for his blessing.
But those aren't things I can write
on that paper.
They aren't things we can
squeeze in.
But there is one thing,
the only other thing I want.
I pick up the pen and write.
Go to the World Series one last time.
Dad takes the notebook from me.
Whispers,
"It's never too late for baseball."

RALLY CAP

I sit up.
Take the hat from my head.
Turn it inside out.
Wear it sideways.
Dad laughs and does the same.
Then Mom.
We all smile.
Real smiles.
Rally cap.
Ready for our comeback.

CLOSER

The big fundraiser
is one week before the Series.
The end of October.
"Cutting it close."
That's what Dan said.
"But people like close.
It feels urgent.
Should force out the crowds.
Plus,
cost will depend on
which stadium,
and by then we'll know
who's playing.
It's going to work out
just fine."
I hope he's right,
because I'm spending
every day
thinking about the World Series,
and that's a lot of hoping
to go to waste.

NO WORD

I haven't heard Jayla's voice since we fought.
I call her,
but she doesn't answer.
Sister Rowan comes by and asks if I want to talk.
She even brings Katy one time.
But I don't have anything to say to them.
The bishop comes by,
but only Mom speaks with him.
The ladies with meals and cards and well wishes
march by.
But all our words are shallow,
meaningless,
not real words at all.
None of us is talking.
Words and thoughts are building up,
crushing me from the inside.
I walk into my closet
and whisper the words
Dad is dying
over
and over again.
And it is only here,
in dark and quiet spaces,
where I can
say it.
Like it's a secret.
My dad is dying.
My dad is dying.
But soon, even whispering it to the dark
isn't enough.
I need more.

GROUP THERAPY V

Share time
is not usually something
the lifers participate in.
Usually we write notes through it.
Play tic-tac-toe,
or draw comics of Ms. Holmes
with her frowny smile.
How can someone have a frowny smile?
It may sound impossible,
but Ms. Holmes has mastered it.
This time, though,
when Ms. Holmes opens up the circle
to talk about anything bothering us,
I raise my hand.
Hear the lifers
gasp.
I don't look at them when I stand up.
I clear my throat
and say the thing I've whispered to the dark.
"My dad is dying."
I nod to Blaine.
"Faster than usual.
Too fast."
I pause.
Can I really take off my armor here?
In front of the lifers?
And these other kids—
basically strangers—
and Ms. Holmes's smile frown?
Deep breath.
"I'm really, really scared."

LIFER SUPPORT

There's a hand on my shoulder,
and it's Blaine's.
He nods.
"I'm scared too."

Two arms around my waist,
squeezing
until I can't breathe.
Jazz's voice is squeaky.
"It's like having spiders
crawling all over your face
every day."

Elena stands to the side,
her arms folded.
She steps closer.
"A lot of days I forget,
but when I remember
it's like running into a wall."

"A wall of spiders," Jazz whispers,
still hugging me tight.

Who knew taking off our armor
would be the bravest thing of all?

WEDNESDAY ALONE

"Not going to the zoo today?"
Mom asks me
a little after breakfast.
I shake my head
but say nothing else.
It's not just that Jayla and I
aren't speaking.
It's more that even if we weren't
fighting,
I would only see
what isn't there anymore.
Hazel.
Why would I go to the zoo
to visit a hole
in my heart?

READING

The night before Dad's supposed to
go back—
back to Hope Circle—
to a different kind of poison
and to Dr. Barry,
I pick up that lonely book of scripture
again
and take it to Mom and Dad's room where he's
packing up.
"Want to take this?" I ask,
remembering how he used to say
scripture made him feel as if
everything would be okay.
Dad throws a pair of socks
into his bag,
takes the book,
and puts it on his nightstand.
"Thanks, Cass.
But I don't think
I'll need it."
I don't know how to tell him
without starting a fight
that I think he does.

THE SPACE BETWEEN

Everyone always wants to know how long
Dad has.
Like they're trying to measure
the space between the words
malignant
and
dead.
Like it really matters.
So what if one space is
longer than another.
Does that suddenly make it okay?
It doesn't change the fact that
dead
is coming.
That cancer
is winning.
That Dad
is losing.
That I
am losing
Dad.
You can't really measure that space.
Those two words
are like walls
inching closer and closer together.
You're stuck,
and it slowly gets harder
to breathe,
to see,
to feel
anything else.

PROS AND CONS OF GETTING TESTED

Pros

1. It might be good news.
2. I can be part of the elephant study.
3. I will know to do as much as I can and live as much as I can now, before I get sick.
4. I can use it to make decisions. Good ones.
5. ~~If I know, I can practice being brave.~~
6. ~~I'll know to go to the doctor about anything even a little bit weird.~~

Cons

1. It might be more bad news.
2. There's nothing positive about having the gene.
3. If I have the gene, I'll feel sick every time I think about my future.
4. I might use it to make decisions. Bad ones.
5. I will always be scared.
6. Going to the doctor doesn't matter. Dad's still dying.
7. I don't want to live with a time limit.

FUNDRAISER DAY

The day of the fundraiser at Dan's Tires
dawns bright and cold.
The wind has whipped all the flyers off
the telephone poles,
and it whistles past my raw, red ears
as I bike down the street.
Past Jayla's.
Past the flowering cherry tree
with one last leaf still holding on,
clinging to summer.
Mom's with Dad for more blood tests.
But she said she'd stop by
around noon.
The clouds are low and gray.
Dan stands outside his shop.
"Looks like snow," he says.
But he doesn't say
the other thing it looks like.
A day when everybody will
stay home
under blankets,
locked up tight,
not even thinking about
getting new tires,
families with cancer,
or sending a girl and her dad
to the World Series.

WAITING ROOM

Dan leads me to
the waiting room.
Black chairs
near a table of magazines,
a water cooler nearby.
"You can watch from here," he says,
pointing out the windows.
"It's going to be a big day."
I nod
and try
to have faith
that maybe
today
I'll see a miracle.

TICKLE

There's a little tickle
in my throat.
A scratching,
a clearing.
It's nothing.

HOURS

I sit inside the lobby
and watch
as the employees walk around the lot
with nothing to do.
Because hardly anybody shows up.
Not the first hour.
Not the second hour.
Or the third hour, either.
And each hour makes the World Series seem
farther
and farther
away.

TISSUES

The box of tissues
is empty.
I know,
because I used them all.

PHONE CALL

My phone vibrates in my pocket.
I reach to grab it, read it.
Jayla.
"Hello?" I say as fast as my fingers
can accept the call.
"How's it going?" she asks without any introduction.
Just the way best friends do,
like we hadn't fought at all.
"Not good. Nobody's come yet."
She sighs.
"I was afraid of that.
They announced the wrong date
at church on Sunday.
I didn't realize it till we got home."
She pauses,
waiting for me to say something.
But what is there to say
when the only thing I want in the whole wide world
is slipping away?
"Have you looked outside?" she asks.
I look again, even though I've been doing that
all morning,
and I see the first few flakes of snow
falling on my fundraiser.
"Don't you worry," says Jayla, like she can hear
me seeing it through the phone.
"I'm going to make a few calls."

HOT

Someone's blasting the heat
so it feels like summer,
and I've got to peel off all my layers
one by one,
until I'm too cold.
Layer them back on.
Do it again.

Sanitize my hands.
Say a prayer.

ONE HOUR LATER

One hour later
Jayla's family pulls up
in their Toyota.
Her dad motions through his window.
One new set of tires.
Dan and his employees
get to work.
Jayla comes inside,
sits next to me,
says,
"I'm sorry about your dad."
"Thanks. We're still
hoping . . ."
The words I do not say
fill every corner of the room.

For a miracle.

But I don't need to say those words
because Jayla already knows.
She reaches in her bag
and pulls out a paper elephant.

I'M SORRY

I clear my throat
and hold that elephant,
careful not to crinkle it.
"I'm sorry," I say.
"For what I said about Alex."
She looks at me.
"It's okay.
He's my brother.
I know that sometimes . . ."
Jayla shrugs,
then her eyes take on
a touch of metal.
"But he's
my
brother."
We hug each other,
and I whisper,
"I know.
You don't have to ex-Spain."

HONK

Jayla's dad honks the horn.
"I have to go," she says.
"Don't leave me," I beg.
"Don't leave me all alone."
"You won't be alone," says Jayla.
"Not for long.
I promise."

CARS (PART I)

At first
it's a trickle—
a slow and steady
drip,
drip,
drip
of cars.
New sets of tires,
or folks picking up
an extra spare.
Some come inside
to say hello.
Sister Rowan is one of the first.
She brushes Cheerio dust off her pants,
laughs,
and gives me a hug.
"Good luck today," she says.
A car pulls up—
one I recognize—
and out jumps Mom.

FORGIVENESS

She walks in and gives me a squeeze.
"Oh, Cass, you're burning up.
Take off your coat, honey."
She laughs.
"How's it going?"
I shrug.
She leans down and whispers,
"I am so proud of you, Cass.
This—
all of this—
it's amazing.
Just like you.
You're amazing.
I want you to know that.
I see you, Cass,
and everything you're becoming.
And I'm so,
so
proud."
I give Mom a hug.
It's one of those hugs
that's more than holding someone close.
The kind where our hearts connect
and whisper to each other,
I will always take care of you.

CARS (PART II)

When I finally pull away I say,
"I don't think it will be enough."
Mom shakes her head.
"Have you looked outside lately?"
She leads me out the door
and past the building
to gaze down the street
at the line of cars,
going back half a mile at least.
Boys on the sidewalk
in baseball caps
holding bright posters
with arrows pointing the way.
Jack, Edison, Maxwell.
Three other familiar faces
weave in between cars,
holding plates filled with goodies.
I hear Elena call out,
"Zucchini bread!
Who wants zucchini bread?
Somebody! Anybody!"
It's a surge,
a flood,
a heavy storm
of love,
friendship,
and caring,
sending us all the way
to the World Series.

EVERYONE

Apparently every single person from church
remembered they need
new tires,
and all their friends need
new tires, too,
after Jayla pulled out the directory
and started calling
everyone
on the list.
It's the sort of thing
best friends do.

HUGGING MAXWELL BACK

I never called
or texted
Maxwell back.
It didn't seem important
and sort of slipped my mind
with everything else happening.
That is
until he walks into Dan's Tires,
wraps his arms around my waist,
and hugs me so hard
I feel like I can't breathe.
"Max," his mom says. "Not so tight."
Max lets go.
"Sorry."
"It's okay," I say.
"That's what you do on a team,
right?"
"Right," he replies.
And then I hug him back.

NO SNIFFING

I try not to sniffle
while Mom is here.
She hates that sound.
I just wipe my nose on my sleeve.
Gross.
She's so busy shaking hands,
she doesn't even notice.
Mom leaves
to check on Dad while he rests.
She's said *hello*
and *thank you*
and *this means so much to us*
so many times,
I think she wants a rest too.
She squeezes me one last time
before going.
Says, "I'll be here at five to bring you home."
I hold back a cough
and say goodbye.

SNOW

Around three o'clock
the snow gets worse. Big, wet flakes
cover the cars.

SUCCESS

About four o'clock,
Dan comes into the lobby.
"I'm declaring this an unmitigated success.
Congratulations
and thank you."
I take
a wadded-up tissue from my pocket
and blow my nose.
"Thank you."
But my voice comes out
garbled
and rough.
"Uh-oh," says Dan.
"It sounds like you're getting a cold."
And just like that,
the fundraiser goes
from success
to disaster.

A COLD

I think of Blaine.
Alone in his room.
His mom in a hospital.
A cold can kill my dad.
So when Dan offers
to give me a ride
home,
I shout,
"No!"
That's the one place
I can't go now.

SAFE

We need
private
box
seats
to keep Dad away from
everyone.
It's
others
who are supposed to be dangerous.
Not me.
What good are
box
seats
now,
if Dad shares them
with me?

They'll understand.
I can get medicine.
It will be okay.
The World Series isn't
lost.

We can't go.
Not now.
I'll kill Dad.
I can't go to the Series.
I can't get in a car with Mom.
I'll get her sick too.
I can't go home.

No. Not home.
Not yet.
If I act fast,
there's still hope.
I just
need
medicine.

Nurse Heather.
The train station
is just
up the hill
and down a few blocks.
It leads right to Hope Circle.
She can help me.

RIDING FOR A CURE

I grab my bike
from the rack outside.
The snow is really coming down now,
in dizzying drafts,
swirling,
blowing against the sides of buildings.
"Hold on," says Dan.
"Your mom will be here soon."
He doesn't understand.
That's the problem.
She'll probably have Dad with her.
I can't let that happen.

There's no time to lose.
Early bird catches
the worm.
Prevention is better
than treatment.
Don't let it get
any worse.

Put on my helmet,
fasten the straps.
No risks.
Safety will keep me
alive.

I pedal across wet sidewalks
away from the line of cars,
away from Dan's Tires,
away from hoping for
the World Series.
And pedal toward
hoping
not to kill Dad.

BIKING IN SNOW

Floating.

Flying.

Flakes   falling

faster,   faster,

faster,   faster.

Spinning.   Soaring.   Spiraling.

Swirling.   Sifting

swiftly,   swiftly,

swiftly,   swiftly.

Hurry,   hurry,

hurry,   hurry.

Slush, slush, slush, slush, slush, s
                                          l
                                            i
                                              p.

FISHTAILING

The cars go slowly, like me.
My back tire fishtails.
Stop to cough.
One block.
Stop to cough.
Two blocks.
Stop at the crosswalk.

INTERSECTION

Half-melted snow covers the road.
Cars whizz by.
Splatter.

Push the button,
push the button,
push the button.

All I get is the
big
red
hand.
But I can't sit here waiting,
and
nobody
is
coming
right now.

It will turn.
The light will change.
Best to be safe
for sure.

Check my watch—
four thirty.
I have to get there
before five.

This light can't last more than
what?

Two minutes?
Not worth the risk.

I'm running,
running,
running out of time.
This street is quiet.
I'll be fine.

But the ice and . . .

No more waiting.

Snow . . .

Go.

I push off the sidewalk,
pedal across the road.
Horn honks.
A truck barrels out of nowhere.
Slams into a car.
The car stopped at the light.
The car ten feet away from me.
Sends it sliding on the ice.

Scream! *Crash! Crunch!*

And I'm thrown back
into slush
and road
and black.

HOME

It's the
BEEP   *BEEP*   *BEEP*
that lets me know
I'm at my home
away from home.
It's the pain that burns
up
and down
my side
that makes it clear
this isn't Hope Circle,
and the person in the hospital bed
is me.

AWAKE

Eyelids flutter.
Light is bright.
Close eyes again,
close them tight.
"Cass?" someone says.
"Cass?"
I moan
and try again
to look.
"She's awake!"
It's Mom.
"Oh, my heavens!
She's awake!"

"Stay away," I croak.
"I'm sick."

Mom puts her arm across my chest,
leans her head against mine.
Tears falling on my face.
"I don't care, Cass.
I don't care."

FOR THE PAIN

Broken arm,
broken ribs,
scrapes and bruises,
concussion—
two days in a coma.
But now I'm awake,
alive,
and the pain won't let me
listen to Mom
as she cries and talks.
Or pay attention
to the cards and flowers
that fill the room.
So when the nurse shoots something
into my IV and says,
"This will help with the pain,"
I only understand
that the room is floating,
and I am falling
down,

       down,

          down.

IN DREAMS

I see Jayla
in a haze
in front of what looks like
Old Faithful.
Water shooting into the air.
She waves me over,
holds up a camera.
One of the old-fashioned kind
that prints the picture right away.
She snaps a photo of us,
and out comes
a postcard.

Did we do it?
Are we really here
together?

BEDSIDE

The next time I wake up
there's a hand on my bedrail.
Big and white
with shiny round knuckles.
"Dad?" I whisper.
He looks up from his book—
the blue book
with gold writing on the cover.
The book of scriptures he's
left unopened the past few months.
"Cass," he whispers back.
"Cass."
His words choke
and wheeze
through the mask he wears
to keep out germs.
"You're reading again," I croak.
He closes the book.
"I am.
That's what happens when you see
a miracle."

MIRACLE

I should have died.
That's what Dad
and the EMTs
and the woman driving
the car
all said.
But I didn't.
Because I was wearing my helmet,
and *it* cracked against
the cement
instead of my head.
The car that slid
and ran into me
was pushed
by the truck that lost control.
That truck
skated through the intersection
and crashed
right into the place on the sidewalk
where I
should have been waiting
to cross.
"How did you know?"
asks Dad.
"How did you know
you needed to cross
even though it wasn't time?"
I shrug,
wince,
say, "I don't know."

Because how do I tell him
it was the two sides of me—
two paths,
living
and dying—
that saved my life?
He smiles and says, "It was God."

If God is in charge of
life
and death,
then I guess he's right.

FRIENDS

People stream through the doors
of my room
like a river.
Some of them I know,
some I don't.
They all wear masks
and gloves,
because Dad refuses to leave my side.
Each one of them leaves behind
one,
two,
ten,
twenty
paper elephants.
"For your miracle," they whisper.
They touch my hand,
wave at Dad.
Nurses,
doctors,
Coach,
Jack,
Maxwell,
the lifers,
Sister Rowan,
the girls from church.
As people move
in
and out
of my little room,
I think about
everyone here.

People who might not be
as much a part of my life
without cancer
holding open the door
and letting them in.

And for the first time
in a long time
I feel

lucky.

HAPPY

"Are you happy, Dad?"
He kisses me. "I'm always
happy with you, kid."

I AM HOPE

Jayla's dad walks in without Jayla or Alex,
which seems odd at first.
But then he hands me an envelope.
"I thought
maybe
you'd like to have this."
It makes a noise when I tip it.
I slide my thumb under the tape
and pour out the contents.
A silver chain slithers into my lap
followed by a
soft *clunk*.
A tiny, metal elephant
with her trunk turned up.
"It's beautiful," I say.
He points to the elephant.
"The upturned trunk means good luck
in some cultures.
And I know that for you . . ."
He doesn't finish his sentence.
He doesn't have to.
He knows that I know that
elephants have twenty copies
of the cancer-fighting p53 gene.
Elephants are luck—
hope—
things that I
finally realize
I have.

THE REAL HOPE CIRCLE

That evening the visitor flood has thinned
to nothing,
and everyone is gone.
Mom comes in and puts a finger
to her lips.
She lights a tiny tea light,
takes one of my hands and one of Dad's.
Dad and I finish the connection.
And when I look at us, I realize that this
is the real hope circle.
The candle flickers
and flutters,
almost goes out, but comes back,
lighting our hands,
holding tight.
Holding on.
Because we'll have
each other
as long as we have
each other.
Not a moment more or less.
And for the first time, I understand
that is enough.

ALEX AND JAYLA

Alex and Jayla come to visit in the afternoon.
Alex smiles behind his mask—
I can tell from his eyes.
Says, "Cass, did you know light
is both a wave and a particle
depending what you're looking for?"
I shake my head and watch as Jayla
takes his hand
and they both sit next to me.
"We're glad you're okay," she says.
Alex pulls his hand away from Jayla.
"Cass. Listen to me.
I was wrong.
You're not Schrödinger's cat.

You're light.

I was thinking about it—
about you—
all wrong.
You're two different things at once,
but they're both good.
They're both you."

BPM

Now Alex holds my hand.
"I'm sorry."
And I feel the softness,
like I finally see him.
All his simplicity
and confusion
bundled up into something
that can only be Alex.
Alex, who always has a solution
and the right thing to say,
and the wrong thing to say,
and who doesn't seem to care
either way.
He looks around the room
and at my monitor.
"Your heart rate is seventy-eight beats per minute.
Seventy-nine.
Ninety-two.
Ninety-six."
Beats per minute,
beats per minute,
beats per minute.

STILL GOING

Jayla leans over
the bed. "Are you still going
to the World Series?"
My heartbeat slows a little.
I smile a great-big real smile.

THE SERIES

I've thought a lot about the Series.
Dan from Dan's Tires
sent three bouquets of flowers,
a giant heart-shaped balloon,
and a small purple teddy bear
to my hospital room.
But there's no changing
Series tickets.
The doctors say
I'm in no condition to go,
and no fundraiser in the world
can change that.
But
I realized those private
box
seats
aren't good only for
fancy people
or sick people.
They're good for people like Alex too.
People who need to get there
early
and stay
late,
until all the crowds leave
and the noise dies down.
Somewhere walled off,
quiet,
safe.

So I talked to Mom
and she called Dan,
and Dan called Jayla's mom,
and Jayla's mom called me.
They've never gone
anywhere like this before,
and now they will.
All the simple and confusing,
proud and embarrassed
parts of them
are going to the World Series.
And this time
Jayla will be the one
sending me
a postcard.

EUREKA (PART II)

Both their mouths hang open
as I tell them.
"Eureka!" says Alex.
I laugh. "Eureka."
Jayla hugs me and whispers,
"Kenya get a better best friend
than you?
I don't think so."
"I was thinking," I whisper to her.
"Maybe we could go somewhere.
Soon.
Like next year.
It doesn't have to be far or foreign.
Just far
enough.
I was thinking
maybe
Old Faithful."
Jayla smiles.
"Sounds like a plan."

NURSE HEATHER

Nurse Heather
walks into
my room the
next evening.
Puts a chair
by my bed.
Asks if it's
okay if
she sits there.
I nod, and
she sits down.
"Are you still
making your
pros-and-cons
list?" she asks.
I shrug and
then tell her.
"I'm not sure
what to write
anymore.
What to want
anymore.
What's a pro?
What's a con?
I feel like
I'm running
out of time
but still have
all the time
in the world."

Nurse Heather
smiles and wipes
away tears.
"If you ask
me, that's life,
whether or
not you have
cancer genes.
Dying and
wishing you
had more of
everything—
time,
fun,
love—
that happens
to us all.
Living and
learning that
what you thought
you wanted
isn't what
you want at
all? You're not
alone with
that one, Cass."

TRADITION

"Dad," I say
during a moment when Mom is out
finding something to eat.
He leans forward.
"Yes, Cass?"
"Tell me something I don't know."
"I love you."
"I already know that."
He shakes his head.
"No. You don't understand.
I love you
so much
it hurts.
I will always,
always,
always love you.
No matter where I am."
I nod.
Because I understand
what he's saying.
"Me too," I whisper.
"Forever and ever."

THE LIST

Everything that was in my pockets
on the day of the accident
is in a plastic bag on the table next to me.
I pull my pros-and-cons list from the bag,
smooth it out,
and read.
Then I crumple it up
and throw it away.
Because I'm not scared anymore
about which future will be mine.
I have one future.
It will be filled
with firsts
and lasts
and a long
enough,
beautiful middle.
Like a book I want to never end
but has to,
because all books do.
When I finally get to the last page
and still want
more,
more,
more,
I don't get mad that the book
isn't longer.
I thank it for
a wonderful story,
lay it down softly

and move on.

467

TEST

"I'm ready," I tell Mom
when she walks in.
"I'm ready to know."
And I don't have to say
anything else.

And   it's
    time   for
        both   sides—
            dying   and living—
                to come   together
                    and   for
                    me to be
                    just
                    me.

One traveler.

BLOG POST

"I'm ready to write that blog post
now," I tell Dad.
The word still feels strange
in my mouth.
Ready.
Scary
and true
all at once.
So Dad hands me the laptop,
and I type slowly
because I can use only one hand.

I write about knowing
and not knowing.
About how I think cancer might kill me,
and a car almost did.
I write about my dad
and elephants.
About light and hope.
And I finally finish with this:

There are two sides of me.
But that isn't anything new.
Everyone
is walking this great, wide world
with all their opposites
filling up the corners of their lives.
We're all living.
We're all dying.
And maybe that's the biggest miracle
of all.

POETRY IN THE HOSPITAL

My last night in the hospital,
Dad sits by my bed and asks,
"Would you like to read a poem?"
I would.
And so he begins to read.

"'Barter,' by Sara Teasdale.
'Life has loveliness to sell,
All beautiful and splendid things,
Blue waves whitened on a cliff,
Soaring fire that sways and sings,
And children's faces looking up
Holding wonder like a cup.'"

LIFE

I think I finally understand that
life
doesn't happen only during
the big things.
Life is not only words like
birth,
marriage,
first,
last,
positive,
negative,
terminal,
death.

Life happens in the spaces,
the places
in between.

Sitting under a favorite tree.
Looking up at the planets and stars.
Reading a favorite book.
Laying my head on my dad's shoulder,
his cheek pressed against my hair.
A best friend's smile.
Riding my bike with the wind in my face.
A perfectly timed silly email.
Standing up and saying something brave.
It's the moment of forgiving someone all the way
and holding them close enough to feel
their heartbeat.

It's hearing the beep of hospital machines
and knowing I'm still here
even though I shouldn't be.
It's a poem that heals a heart,
and a line of cars around the block.
It's a thousand paper elephants in a hospital room.
It's hopes
and dreams
and stories

and miracles.

EPILOGUE

There's a hill you have to climb
before you can bike across the Golden Gate Bridge.
Two miles of pedaling
against the wind.
We got to the end of the ride—
tired,
out of breath,
legs burning.
I wanted to throw myself onto the grass.

But Dad wouldn't let me.
He spun me around,
showed me how far we had come.
"Was it worth it?" he asked.
"Worth it," I replied.
He hugged me.
"The view at the end
always is."

AUTHOR'S NOTE

The events in this book are truer than I would like them to be. The genetic condition Cass's dad has is real. It is called Li-Fraumeni syndrome, and it is passed down through families and demolishes them. Scientists used to think that only four hundred families worldwide had this rare condition. But with more genetic testing, they now think that somewhere between one in five thousand families and one in twenty thousand families has the condition. Half the people with Li-Fraumeni syndrome develop cancer before the age of forty and battle it off and on for the rest of their lives. Some studies have found women with LFS have a 50 percent chance of cancer by age thirty due to their increased risk of breast cancer.

That is not the only true part of this book. Elephants really do have twenty copies of the p53 gene, the very gene that is mutated in people with Li-Fraumeni syndrome. A doctor, scientist, and researcher named Dr. Joshua Schiffman studies elephants at the Hogle Zoo in Salt Lake City, Utah, and at the Center for Elephant Conservation in Polk City, Florida, to try to discover the secrets of elephant DNA and how it might help humans. The work he does is important to all those who suffer from Li-Fraumeni syndrome.

Other parts of this story are based on actual places, people, and elephants. My brother-in-law Chris Greenman had Li-Fraumeni syndrome, and he died in 2017 from osteosarcoma. He battled it for two years with my sister and my niece (who also has the gene) by his side. Many of the poems in this story are based on pictures and moments and words they said. Too many. Chris received treatment at the Huntsman Cancer Institute in Salt Lake City. The road outside the institute is called "Circle of Hope." The Hogle Zoo in Salt Lake City really was home to the oldest elephant in North America. Her name was Dari. She died in 2015 and had the most beautiful orange eyes. Just like a sunset during a forest fire.

And of course all the books Cass checks out are real. The poems her dad reads are real. The science that Alex spouts is real.

And life is real. It really is. And it's beautiful.

ACKNOWLEDGMENTS

I began writing *The Hope of Elephants* in a cramped hotel room in Salt Lake City as I was caring for my niece while her mom and dad were at the hospital for chemo treatments. That was in 2015. When you work on a book for seven years, it's very easy to forget someone who helped along the way, and I apologize in advance if I left your name off here. I promise, it's not because I'm not deeply appreciative.

The following people read this story and gave me fantastic feedback (even if that feedback was just loving it). Thank you to Jamie Pacton, Jessica Vitalis, Joy McCullough, Kit Rosewater, Cory Leonardo, Katniss Hinkel, Sheena Boekweg, Heather Murphy Capps, Julie Artz, Jennifer Ray, Ellie Terry, Rachel Lynn Solomon, Anne Appert, Shar Abreu Peterson, and Nicole Panteleakos.

Thank you to my agent, Elizabeth Harding, for your direction and advocacy, and to my editor, Karen Boss, for loving this story the way I do and letting it remain mine.

A special thanks to Cindy Baldwin, who was not just my first reader but my biggest cheerleader, and who held hope for me when I couldn't hold it for myself.

Thank you to my mom for reading and loving this book in one of its earliest forms. Mom's approval always means the world!

Thank you to my husband, who listened to portions of this book several times over the years, even though he really hates sad stories.

All my love to Darci and Eliza Greenman. Thank you for letting me plunder your heartache for poetry. I hope it has done your own story a small amount of justice.

And finally, thank you to God. Mostly for not striking me with lightning for what I said to you when my heart was breaking and then for helping me turn that pain into something (hopefully) beautiful.